SPECTRA

notionpress
.com

SPECTRA

Lolita Jude

notionpress.com

Notion Press

5 Muthu Kalathy Street, Triplicane,

Chennai - 600 005

First Published by Notion Press 2014

ISBN: 978-93-84381-31-8

Dedicated To My Family

Chris, Naina & Palakh

AUTHOR'S NOTE

The mind can spin yarns far beyond reality. That is the beauty of fiction. It adds that extra spice to life and makes it interesting. I have always had a very fertile imagination. It stood me in good stead all through my student days and continues to keep me as young as I want to be. It is important to let the child in us surface every once in a while and remember our truant moments; when we played a prank on someone or how we wheedled out of a difficult situation. I have written 'Spectra' my first novella for children. In reading this book, dear children, I am sure you will realize that nothing is impossible if you set your mind to it. No goal is unattainable we only have to look for the means to achieve it.

I'd like to thank my beautiful family: My husband, Chris, who is my anchor and my in-house editor-in-chief and my daughters Naina and Palakh for their support and encouragement.

I have enjoyed writing this book for you. I hope you enjoy reading it too.

LOLITA JUDE

CHAPTER 1

It was the last day of school before my summer holidays began. I had worked really hard the entire year and I was glad to have a break from school work. My school had recently been accredited as one of the top ten schools in the county. The Principal and teachers told us that it was on account of our diligence and sincerity as students that the school had achieved this honour. As a reward, we were granted a vacation, free of assignments and summer projects. I went to the same school as my friends: Jude, Dom, Cara and Mignonne. As we were in different classes, we had decided to meet in the cafeteria after school to discuss our plans for the holidays. We had formed a club called the 'Aces Club' and we had promised ourselves that we would enjoy every bit of our 'homework-free' holidays.

We lived in a small, peaceful town, where our great-grandparents had settled in years ago. The population was only around three hundred. What made our town different from other small towns was the fact that we were self-sufficient. We had every modern amenity that the most advanced metropolis boasted of and yet, we had managed to keep our town away from the temptations of the world. We had a fine education system and the children of the town were given the freedom and opportunity to choose and pursue a career of their choice. Our great-grandparents were very enterprising and had managed to make this little town of ours, a fabulous place to live in. We had two sister towns adjoining ours and were separated from each other by the indent of land and sea.

As we lived along the coast, the climate was equable. The countryside was very picturesque as each of our town's residents had their own beautiful, landscape gardens, surrounding their spacious homes. It was especially lovely at this time of the year as all the trees were laden with colourful blossoms. It was almost as if we lived in a world of our own. We were content to enjoy our holidays in this little town of ours even though at times the temperature rose to almost 40 degrees Fahrenheit. However, we did not mind the summer heat because we had every possible modern amenity and our

'Country Club' had a number of indoor games to keep us occupied whenever the temperature rose higher.

This summer we were sure we would enjoy ourselves more than usual as my friends and I had fared brilliantly in school and our parents were very proud of our grades. They had given each of us a huge allowance as they felt we deserved the reward for our commitment to our school work. We wanted to make the most of this holiday and had promised ourselves that this year our 'Aces Club' would flourish. We got back home that day all excited and eager to put our plans into action. The beach was very close to where we lived and we had decided to meet there the following morning at 6:00 a.m. We waved goodbye promising to be punctual.

I could hardly sleep with excitement! I set the alarm clock for 5:00 a.m. I also assured that my friends had done the same.

The next morning I was up, long before the alarm clock went off. I showered, dressed and was all set for the beach with my backpack filled with the yummiest of food. I met Jude, Cara and Mignonne on the way as they lived next door. Jude had brought along his cricket bat, stumps and a beach umbrella, Cara had carried her amazing collection of comic books and Mignonne had her bag full of 'gadgets' with her. She was nicknamed 'Gadget Princess' by us.

"Hey Veronica!" shouted Dom, "Wait for me!"

"Okay." I yelled back.

As always, Dom was the last to arrive so obviously, he travelled light. We made a merry party, the five of us, each one of us was unique in our own special way yet, we got along famously. In a trice, we reached the beach and before you could say 'Jack Robinson', the boys had set up the 'pitch' for our cricket match.

Jude and Cara were the most responsible, so they took charge. They kept our belongings in a safe place near the rocks. We began our match. I was the umpire, commentator, score-keeper, caterer, all rolled-in-one. The match began. Mignonne was the youngest, but could take on the boys any day. Cara was a tom-boy, athletic and long limbed and could field like nobody else could. Dom may have been laid back about punctuality but, with a bat in hand he was the most formidable of all. Jude was a wiz when it came to bowling, so you see; each of my friends had their strengths.

It was almost seven o'clock and our match was well underway, with the boys scoring 50 runs, without losing a wicket. As it was a limited overs match, Cara and Mignonne had to do their utmost to contain the runs or else it would be a mammoth task to get back into the game and they did not believe in giving up that easily. Mignonne threw a curved ball and Dom swung his bat, with Cara waiting to catch it. Suddenly, the ball disappeared as if swallowed by thin air. We started looking for it. There was no one else on the beach and the tide was not in so, it was impossible that the ball had gotten lost.

All of us started looking for the ball. Cara had just stumbled upon it, lying ensconced among a pile of round, pebbled stones, when Mignonne gave out a loud cry.

"Come here, can you believe this?" she asked.

Now we all knew Mignonne was famous for her 'discoveries'. We humoured her as she was the youngest. We ran to where she was and believe you me; we reacted the same way. I'm sure you would never guess what Mignonne, had found. No, it was not a litter of pups, or a hidden cave, or even a secret pathway. She had actually found a dazzling diamond. We quickly looked around, to see if anyone had seen us. We knew that this beautiful object would be surely missed and the person, to whom it belonged, would not take kindly to losing such an expensive gem. As quickly as they had set up the pitch, the boys gathered the cricket gear as we picked up our belongings. We managed to cover our tracks and walked briskly towards Dom's home, taking a longer route.

Dom's parents were very generous and made available to us, his special friends, a tree house and a section of the basement of their house. We went to his tree house, which was well and truly hidden, from everyone. Only his parents and we knew it existed. As I mentioned earlier, our parents were very busy. We decided to discuss this amazing find among ourselves before we went to them as they were really hard-pressed for time. The 'diamond' was a very unusual discovery and warranted serious thinking. Jude, our chair-person, had called for an emergency meeting. Cara, who was the secretary, was to take down the minutes and Mignonne, Dom and I, the worthy members of our 'Aces Club', would contribute by voicing our opinion at the meeting.

"This calls for very serious thinking," said Jude, "We need to be very careful and discreet about this unusual find."

We all nodded in agreement. "How are we going to find the owner?" asked Cara.

"Well! This is surely a precious and very expensive gem, so, naturally, the owner will come looking for 'it'." said Jude.

"The most important thing that each of us has to remember is that we cannot, and I mean it, we cannot discuss this with anyone, not even our parents." said Cara.

"Let us refer to it as 'spectra', instead of calling it a gem or a diamond." whispered Mignonne.

"Suits me fine." added Dom.

"We need to keep it in a very safe place so that we do not endanger ourselves." I said

"As always, Veronica, you are right about being cautious rather than being sorry later." said Jude.

"Hey, I know where to hide 'spectra'. A place nobody will EVER think of looking." said Mignonne.

"Where?" shouted everyone in unison.

"Here in this tree house. It is hidden and nobody knows about it except us and Dom's parents." she said. "There's a groove in the branch of this tree which I had carved out a long time ago and even if the tree house is discovered, the person will NEVER find spectra." she added.

Everyone looked at Mignonne in amazement. She was always fixing or carving things.

What had begun as a quiet morning of fun and games had taken on a new dimension altogether. Jude looked around and quickly descended the steps of the tree-house keeping a sharp look-out for suspicious characters, while Mignonne hid spectra. The rest of us also followed suit. We had decided to take turns to keep watch and we had a clear view of the beach from my house. Our parents would not be suspicious of our actions as we often spent time at each others' houses during the vacations.

My sister was at camp for the entire vacation, so I had the room all to myself. Jude and I took turns first. We looked at the entire expanse of the beach through our field-glasses. There were many children and their parents but nobody who was a stranger to us. As you are aware, we lived in a small, peaceful town so, everybody knew each other. An hour went by in this manner. Jude needed to run some errands for his mum so he left and said he'd be back after lunch. We had asked Dom, Cara and Mignonne to join us after lunch. I had not slept the previous night, so I thought of taking a short nap before they came over.

We had a quick meeting and came up with a strategy to discreetly deal with the matter in hand without arousing any suspicion. Cara and Mignonne had asked their parents' permission to stay the night. We decided to take turns and watch-out for any unusual activity during the night. So began our quest for the stranger who had lost or stolen spectra. It was going to be a long, exciting night! I decided to take the first watch, as I had already rested earlier and in my excitement, I would not be able to sleep anyway. What I had not envisaged was how every sound seemed more magnified in the dark and the silence of the night! The crickets sounded louder than ever, the sound of the wind passing through the trees made me startle more than once. Other than these eerie night sounds nothing eventful happened during my watch.

Soon it was Cara's turn. The best quality that Cara has is that she can occupy herself for hours on end doing something creative. She kept her eyes glued on the beach as well as fashioned a new logo for our club. Mignonne took her turn next; she worked out a schedule wherein we would be able to document everything in an 'incognito account'.

In the morning, we did not have much to report except for the fact that all of us were frightened more on account of the strange night sounds and that none of us had heard or observed any suspicious activity. We also realized that we were not as brave as we thought we were.

CHAPTER 2

We had told the boys we'd meet them at the tree-house after breakfast. I made pancakes and we gobbled three each and packed the rest for the boys in a Tupperware box. I also carried my backpack of goodies. We arrived at the tree-house at the same time as the boys. Dom had set up the surveillance system in such a manner that it covered that part of the beach where we had found spectra and the access road to the beach. After the boys had wolfed down all the pancakes, we started viewing the recording. Again, there was no strange person or activity and the only fact we established was that the person who had lost or stolen spectra had not yet realized that it was missing.

We all agreed that it was necessary to keep watch during the day as well. The boys took their turn this time and Cara, Mignonne and I, went to the 'Country Club' to swim and play a game of basketball. We had to improvise for though we had made many plans as a team for the holidays, this unexpected development meant we had to work out a different schedule. It was far too exciting a prospect and had really given us a lot to think about at the beginning of our holidays.

After a nail-biting finish to our basketball game which we won against some of our neighbours' kids, we went to our respective houses to shower and have lunch and then assemble at my house. It was now Jude and Dom's turn to go to the Country Club and enjoy themselves. The boys had a cricket match scheduled for that afternoon. It was almost unheard of among our neighbours that the five of us ever went to the Country Club without each other. The boys decided to make up some excuse for our absence. We followed the same modus operandi as the previous day. I took a nap while Cara and Mignonne updated the incognito account. They also took turns in watching the news and scanned the newspaper for any reports regarding spectra. Once again, there was nothing that gave us a lead.

Jude and Dom joined us at 7p.m. and were as jubilant that they had won their match as were we on winning ours. After a while, the discussion veered towards spectra. Something did not quite seem right. We were certain that spectra was rare and precious but why had nobody come to look for it was what had us flummoxed. However, we decided to continue our turns at keeping watch and a sharp look out for strangers. The boys were about to leave when suddenly Mignonne, who was very pensive till now, gave out a cry. We ran to her side and asked her what had happened.

"Hey, what if, we go back to the spot we found spectra tomorrow at 6 a.m.?" she asked.

"Whatever for?" we all yelled back in unison.

"Pretty please," she implored, making her famous 'puppy face'. "You will not be sorry, I promise." she added.

"Okay." said Jude.

"We are subjecting ourselves to a considerable amount of risk." I said.

"We can ask Dom to stay back and keep watch. He can warn us if he sees any stranger." said Mignonne, her large eyes wide with excitement.

Dom told us that he was more than happy to stay back and watch the beach. Our only concern was that he should stay awake and not fall asleep. He was not a morning person and knowing that we could not expect him to be alert. Cara came to the rescue by offering to keep watch with him. With that settled, we bid the boys goodbye and continued with the watch. Except for the eerie night sounds we did not have anything new to report. All of us looked forward to the morning. Mignonne was barely able to sleep in her excitement.

CHAPTER 3

The next day, we were up way before time. We walked with Cara to Dom's house. Dom was actually awake and ready with his gear all set to keep watch. We waved goodbye and set off at a brisk pace to the beach. Mignonne was very quiet and we knew that she had something really big in store for us. It was only on such occasions that she kept quiet. She was the most talkative of us. We reached the beach. With bated breath and asking us to watch the pathway to the beach, she went to the spot we had found spectra. She gave out a sharp cry.

"Just as I thought," she said. "I knew it must have been something to this effect." she added.

Jude and I rushed to her side. Our jaws almost dropped to the floor at the sight we saw! Now as you may recall Mignonne was famous for her gadgets. She happened to have left behind one of her contraptions neatly buried in the sand while we were all inspecting spectra.

On asking her what made her do that she said, "I had a hunch about this."

You would never guess what was in that contraption. Mignonne deftly took out the box she had buried and once again covering our tracks we went to the tree house. Dom and Cara were there and they reported that they had not seen a single soul on that stretch of the beach. In fact, it was too early for most people to wake up as it was holiday time.

Mignonne asked Dom to lay out a sheet and then opened the box she had buried. Dom and Cara also reacted the way we did. Did you guess why? Well, the box had managed to trap many more 'diamonds' and other precious jewels in it.

"This is too big for us to handle," said Jude. "We need to go to our parents and the authorities." he added.

"Yes, you are right." said Cara. We all nodded our heads in agreement.

"We will just have to wait till it is 9 a.m. and then we can tell them." said Jude.

Then all of us turned to Mignonne. "How did you know about the other jewels?" We asked in amazement.

"Well," she said, "You know how I had found spectra right? It was stuck in a little groove. So I had a theory but, I was not sure. That made me put in the box and cover it in such a way that nobody would come across it. You were busy examining spectra wondering whether it was real so that gave me enough time to place the box."

We all looked at her, wonderstruck.

"You really are brilliant." said Cara.

Mignonne's face lit up at being praised. Praise from Cara, her sister, meant the world to her.

"Could you please tell us how you thought there would be more jewels?" Cara asked.

"You have not told us that, Mignonne." she said.

"Well, when I picked up spectra from that groove, I spied an opening. I wonder where it leads to though." Mignonne said.

"There is no jewellery shop for miles from here but what has me foxed is how these jewels which are worth so much money have not been missed so far?" she added.

"Jewellery shop?" we all said in unison.

"What makes you think these jewels are from a jewellery store?" asked Cara.

"Think about it. Why has nobody come to claim spectra? Also how is it that the box was full of jewels? Obviously, nobody is aware that this is happening. Or, they do not know where the jewels are disappearing." Mignonne replied.

"Or, there must be something more to it." said Dom in a slow drawl.

"Of course there is, sport!" said Jude. "What is the mystery? Why has nothing been reported?" he added.

"Any theories?" asked Cara.

Nobody answered but all had pensive looks on their faces.

We spent almost a half hour in this fashion. Jude started pacing up and down. Cara went to her notepad and started working on it. Dom started looking at the newspapers. Mignonne was examining the box closely. I decided to bring out the refreshments I had carried. I offered them to my friends saying, "You cannot think on an empty stomach, can you?"

Dom thanked me profusely as he had not had any breakfast up till then. The others gobbled up the snacks without saying anything. Dom casually switched on the television and suddenly there it was! The reporter was mentioning something to the effect of a strange disappearance of jewellery worth millions. The owner had shut shop for a few days till the mystery was solved. She also said that there was no evidence of a break-in or theft. However, there was no reference made to the name of the 'owner' of the jewels. So, there was our breakthrough. The reason nobody had claimed the jewels was because, they had no clue where the jewels had disappeared. To think we had found it and that too while we were playing a regular game of cricket! Thanks to our 'gadget princess' Mignonne, we had perhaps found all the missing jewels. The only important thing we had to ensure was that we returned them to the rightful owner.

Our parents had already left for work by the time we got back home so we decided to keep the box safely in Dom's house and speak with our parents when they returned. We sent them a text message saying that there was a surprise party at Dom's house and they were invited. They replied that they would certainly be available. We also felt the need to inform the local police but thought we would leave that to our parents.

This was so exciting! What a wonderful way to spend our summer vacations!

Mignonne started rubbing her hands in glee. She asked, "Do you think there is a REWARD for the one who finds the jewels?"

"As of now, the owner only knows that his jewels worth millions are missing. He must be grief-stricken by his loss. Perhaps, once he recovers from his shock, he may announce a reward." Cara said in a solemn voice stifling her laughter.

"We can donate the reward money for a worthy cause." Jude added, with a twinkle in his eye.

Mignonne did not receive this news very pleasantly and all of us burst out laughing. We loved to tease Mignonne because she was very trusting.

Now that the mystery was solved, we decided to go to our respective homes and rest as none of us had slept these past days. Dom had a state of the art security system and not just us but the entire town would hear the alarm if it ever went off. He set it up and all of us left knowing very well that the jewels were safe in Dom's house. We were to meet at 6:00 p.m. and there was enough time for us to have a good lunch and a nap. We all set alarms on our cell-phones and also said that we would telephone each other in case someone over-slept. The past few days were far too exciting and we really needed to catch up on our sleep.

The afternoon passed quickly and soon it was time to leave for Dom's house. My parents had returned home by then. They asked me what the occasion was and the reason we had been invited over. My mum recalled that there was no birthday or anniversary that either Dom or his parents were celebrating, anytime soon. I mumbled something about Dom topping his class or something to that effect. Fortunately, the next day was a public holiday and thus the time was right and my parents too, welcomed a change of scene from their hectic schedules. So, they did not ask me any further questions and I was relieved as I did not want to ruin the thrill of narrating the sensational news to them as members of the Aces Club.

We were the first to arrive at Dom's place. Cara, Mignonne, Jude and their parents arrived soon after. We had decided to let Jude lead the conversation. He asked our parents to move to the basement where Dom had 'safely' kept the jewels. Even Dom's basement looked amazing. It had everything one would need if ever stuck in a tornado or storm. He had set up a neat array of refreshments and we were ready to begin. As our parents had just returned from work, we decided we would serve them the food first and then tell them about our great find.

Our parents had very packed schedules and no time to meet up though they were good friends. After half an hour of exchanging pleasantries and updating each other about their work, Jude called their attention to the 'important' matter at hand.

Jude was very thorough when it came to conducting a meeting. He would have every detail planned and an agenda ready. We all told him that he would do fine as the VP of a multi-national organization. He welcomed our parents and told them to brace themselves as they were to hear something really fantastic. He reassured them that none of us were ailing or had got into any trouble. However, the impending news really warranted their guidance and assistance.

Then Jude opened the box and put it out on display.

"Where on earth did you find this?" my mum was the first to exclaim.

"They are not real jewels, dear." was my dad's response.

"Most certainly they are." said our mothers in unison. "We can have them appraised by Mr. Sinclair, our friend. He is an expert." they added.

"Well!" my dad replied, "What do I know of gems and jewels?"

"That's perfectly alright dear; we do not expect you to know everything." My mum said, reassuring him.

My dad was a genius when it came to his work and was held in high esteem by his company. However, he had absolutely no clue when it came to women's clothing or jewellery. As long as the outfit we picked out was high-priced, he considered it to be classy and good. Often, we would add a few digits to the actual price as only then he would consider it to be a good buy. All of us just adored him as he would indulge and fulfill all our whims.

Jude once more called the meeting to order and continued, "We most certainly will establish whether these jewels are real or not, but, what we would like to know is do we go to the police or do we hold on to these jewels for now?"

"Good thinking son." said Jude's dad. "We have to involve the police. In fact, I think I'll contact my friend the Superintendent of Police right away." he said.

"Why don't we ask Mr. Sinclair to meet us at the same time the SP is available?" Dom's dad asked.

"That would be perfect." agreed Jude's dad.

As it was quite late and time for dinner, Jude's dad fixed the meeting for the next day. It was a public holiday so, it was decided that the SP and Mr. Sinclair would join us for lunch at Dom's house. It was going to be a pound party as we did not want to burden Dom's mom with the cooking on her day off.

Our parents were as excited as us. This was something unheard of in our quiet and peaceful town where the biggest news of the day would perhaps be the acquisition of a new pup or kitten. We had a delicious dinner which Dom's mother had cooked for us. It was almost 9:00 p.m. so we bid goodbye to Dom and his parents. His dad locked the box of jewels in his safe and activated the alarms and set up the surveillance system. Dom's house was now as secure as Fort Knox. We knew we had nothing to worry about.

CHAPTER 4

The next morning dawned and it was a beautiful day. The sun was shining, the trees were in full bloom and there was a pleasant sea breeze blowing that evened the summer heat perfectly. All of us headed to the Country Club to play a few games and swim. We had not managed to go there together ever since we had found the jewels. It was really good to finally play the games as the fantastic five because we always aced all of them. After three games of basketball and an hour in the pool, we went back home.

My mum had made my favourite breakfast – French toast. I had my fill and helped my mum make the roast chicken and baked potatoes that we were to take to Dom's place for lunch. For dessert, my mum made another of my favourites – Baked Caramel Pudding. Cara's and Mignonne's mum was to make her famous Greek Salad and baked vegetables. Jude's mum had offered to cook her special dishes as did Dom's mum. We were eagerly waiting to tuck in the delicious lunch. Our parents had strictly warned us that the discussion about our findings would be only after our guests and all of us did justice to the lunch. All of us had hearty appetites and our parents always made sure that we ate well no matter how busy they were at work.

We met at Dom's place and helped set the table. Mr. Sinclair and SP Jensen arrived as the clock struck 1:00 p.m. They thanked our parents profusely for the delicious lunch and after we all had caught up with the small talk and cleared the table; we proceeded to Dom's basement.

Mr. Sinclair had carried his eye-piece and tools to examine the jewels. My mum had told him that she needed him to look at some jewels her late aunt had left her, and have them authenticated and weighed. Dom's dad took out the box from the safe and carried it to the basement. He set it on the large table so that all of us could gather around it and observe while Mr. Sinclair checked the gems. It was important at this stage not to divulge to him exactly where we had found the gems. So, we went along with the other story that my mum had told him of inheriting them.

Mr. Sinclair diligently began his work picking up and examining every gemstone and weighing each one of them. It took almost an hour and a half. It was interesting watching him at work – tabulating his findings and cataloging each gem according to its name, size, cut, carat etc. He was thorough in his appraisal and at the end of the hour and half he had not only examined each and every jewel but, he had also written the price against each of them. I had made a mental calculation while Mr. Sinclair was writing out the price against each gem and it had already amounted to more than a million dollars. It was an exhausting and laborious task so Dom's mum offered Mr. Sinclair and all of us some refreshing orange juice and lightly buttered scones. The last gem was then examined by him and after he had entered the details, he made the final tally and just as I had calculated, it did amount to a little over a million dollars. My mum thanked Mr. Sinclair profusely and invited him to our home for dinner the following week. He accepted the invitation and then left, as he had to meet a friend.

Our friendly Superintendent Jensen, who had been very silent while Mr. Sinclair was evaluating the jewels, walked up to my mum and congratulated her. She told him the jewels did not belong to her. Jude then narrated the entire story to SP Jensen about how we had found 'spectra' and the rest of the gems. Dom also added about the news clip and mentioned the news channel that had reported it. The SP told us that he would begin his investigation and make a few calls to his friends in that precinct. However, he requested Dom's dad to lock up the jewels in the safe along with Mr. Sinclair's appraisal report. Mignonne requested that her box be returned as she was very possessive about her belongings and also because there was a new significance attached to the box. So the contents were transferred to another box which was then duly sealed and locked in the safe. There was another surprise for us which was the most exciting of the events of that day and that was the invitation from the Super for us kids to join him in his investigation!

"Three cheers for the Super, hip, hip hurray!" we shouted.

This was going to be our best summer vacation ever! We were actually going to accompany the SP on a case! How wonderful that was!

The SP gave us badges and instructed us to tell the officers from the other precinct that we had been assigned by our school, to research and write a paper on the working of the police station of the neighbouring precinct. Nobody would ever suspect us, as we were often given several projects for added credits, during our holidays and since each of us had topped our class, it seemed plausible that we would be the ones chosen to lead the project. We were to leave for the precinct at 11:00 a.m. the following morning.

We thanked Dom and his parents for their hospitality and left as we had an early start the next day.

CHAPTER 5

I was up at dawn as were the others. We were very excited and 11:00 a.m. seemed to be a long way off. So, we went to the 'Country Club' and played our usual games. It also would not arouse any suspicion as we always dominated the play and came up with novel ideas which everyone looked forward to. We left at a quarter past ten, which gave us enough time to take a quick shower and tuck in some brunch. SP Jensen was to pick us up from Dom's place so we assembled there by a quarter to eleven. It would be the first time that we were travelling by a police car. We were ecstatic!

The SP had enough to occupy his mind so; we had decided to put on our best behaviour as instructed by our parents. It was an effort to keep silent throughout the journey, especially for Mignonne. That girl could even speak with the walls if none of us were around. Another thing she could not do was to keep a secret. We could well imagine the agony she was going through. Cara had to keep reminding her it was imperative to do so for our safety and security. Mignonne trusted her sister's judgment so she readily complied.

The SP told Jude to take down notes as he questioned the officers and some of the towns-people. Jude diligently did as he was told. Our next stop was the television studio from where the news of the missing jewels had been telecast. We followed the SP's lead and only asked them questions about rare and fantastic happenings in the past week.

The director was very kind and made us very comfortable. He took us to the archives and asked one of his assistants to show us the news footage of the earlier week. As we had noted the day and date when the news of the missing jewels had been telecast, we located the news clip and asked the assistant to copy it for us on a disc, without making it seem obvious. SP Jensen asked a few questions about some other news clips and then casually mentioned the 'missing jewels' clip. The assistant told us he did not know the details as he had been on leave the previous week and had just resumed work. So, he introduced us to the TV Reporter who had covered the case.

She was a vibrant, young lady who was very glad to meet us and was more than obliging to give us details of the owner as well as his address. The SP also took down details of some other unsolved cases so as not to draw attention to this particular case. Jude too made a note of the details in his notepad. We exchanged glances but, none of us said a word. It was very important that we kept the entire operation under wraps as it involved a lot of money. It was now half past one and we all suddenly realized that we were famished. We thanked the director for his time, bid him goodbye and went back to the police car where we had our lunch. Yes, you guessed right, I had carried sandwiches for everyone. Cara had made a delicious mocktail for all of us and we gulped it down happily. SP Jensen told us that he would drop us at Dom's place and would meet us after he finished his day's work at 7:00 p.m.

It had been an amazing morning and we were more exhausted by the excitement than the activity. Cara suggested that we should all go home and take a nap and meet at Dom's place at 6:45 p.m. Our parents were kept updated about the happenings and said they would join us at a quarter past 7:00 p.m., as it was a working day.

The SP arrived and we once more assembled in Dom's basement. Jude's mum had sent some delicious sandwiches for all of us. Dom's refrigerator was always stocked with goodies and fresh fruit juice. We made ourselves comfortable as did our friendly SP Jensen. He asked us what grades we were in and what our plans were for the future. He was a bachelor and was really good with kids and the youth. The towns-people admired his dedication and diligence and were proud that his efforts had kept our small town free of crime. Often, he would help organize tournaments and competitions that kept everyone occupied and our energies channelled in a positive manner. We were like one big, happy family that cared for each other yet, gave each other their own space.

Our parents joined us and the SP told them that it would be sometime before the case was solved. We had established that the jewels had reached our end of the beach by accident. Had it been a pre-meditated theft, the thieves would have come looking for the jewels. How the jewels had made it to the spot? Did they really belong to the jeweller who claimed that he was missing the jewels? Was there anything more to this entire incident? The SP had listed out a whole lot of things that needed to be investigated. He told our parents that as of now, he would take us along but, would stop the instant he felt or sensed there was any danger. The agenda for the next day was discussed and set up and once again we were to ride along with the SP to the neighbouring precinct at 11:00 a.m.

CHAPTER 6

We followed the same routine as the previous day and soon we were on our way, armed with plenty to eat and drink. The first stop was the neighbouring town's police station. The Super had called his friend in the precinct and asked for one of their officers' to accompany us to the jeweller's house. Then it would not arouse any suspicion. It would seem as if the police were following up on the case. We were instructed to stay in the car as we did not want to unnerve the jeweller. The SP was to first establish a rapport and then introduce us as students who had been given a summer project which included field visits.

The jeweller turned out to be quite a nice sort though he seemed very disturbed by his loss. He told us he was about to leave for his showroom. He had still kept his manufacturing unit closed and was only attending to his regular and select clientele. The officer accompanying SP Jensen asked to see the employees' roster from the database and copied the names and addresses onto a pen drive.

The jeweller had asked only his senior employees, employed in the showroom, to report to work ever since the incident. He made arrangements for us to interview them in his office. As the shop was closed for new and prospective clients there were no customers, so we could speak with the employees without any interruptions. However, the employees working in the manufacturing unit had been given leave till further notice. We made a note of their names and addresses as a separate attachment and saved it on SP Jensen's iPad.

We thanked the jeweller for his time and Mignonne in her inimitable way expressed her thanks so genuinely that the jeweller invited us to his home for refreshments. SP Jensen politely declined as did we. However, he informed him that we would be interviewing the other employees who worked in the manufacturing unit. As it was almost lunch-time, we took his leave and after SP Jensen had dropped the officer to the police station, we went to the park nearby and had our delicious lunch. Dom had even carried ice candy in an icebox. After lunch, we set off for home with the promise of another interesting day.

SP Jensen accompanied us to Dom's home so that we could work out a strategy. Yes, it was indeed amazing that our Super was involving us in every part of the investigation! He told us that it was our find and that it was justified that we were involved in every part of the investigation. He was also impressed that we could keep secrets so well.

Jude had a few queries: He said, "Why do we need to interview the employees in the manufacturing unit at this stage? Will it not make them suspicious or put them on their guard?"

"That would in fact give us our lead. Besides, we will have some policemen in plainclothes keeping a check on their movements once we have interviewed them." SP Jensen replied.

"Like a stakeout?" asked Mignonne.

"Yes, dear girl, it will be a stakeout but more of a casual kind." SP Jensen replied. "We have not yet established the nature of the crime as the jewels are in our possession. I would also like to visit the manufacturing unit in a couple of days. For now, let us work on the interviews. Would you like to conduct them Veronica, Cara and Mignonne?" he asked.

"We'd love to." we replied.

"I'll give you a format that you can follow and one of you can also record the interview. I'll give you a tiny recording device that nobody will notice." he added.

"I cannot wait to get started!" said Cara.

We all looked at Cara in surprise. She was the most staid and practical among us and NEVER got carried away.

The boys were informed that they would conduct the interviews the day after we'd conducted ours. SP Jensen then asked us to go about our regular activities as there was nothing more to do that day.

We decided to take a walk on the beach and build some sand castles. Jude, Mignonne and Dom were awesome when it came to building them and Cara was excellent at landscaping. I could only assist them by filling sand in the pails as I was not artistic. It was 6:30 p.m. by the time the castle was ready. It was truly a work of art, beautifully structured with a moat and bridge as well. Cara took pictures of the castle. It had engrossed us so much that we did not realize that so much time had passed. We gathered our things and went to our respective homes. It had been an interesting day and the next day had much more in store for us.

I was out like a light as soon as I had my dinner. I dreamt I was interviewing people from all walks of life – Celebrities, Lawyers, Teachers and several others. I woke up with a start mid-interview. The dream was so vivid; I almost believed it had taken place in reality.

CHAPTER 7

I hurriedly got dressed and had a hasty breakfast as I did not want to be late. We were to make a quick stop at the spot where we had found the jewels and then proceed to the Country Club. Jude had carried his beach umbrella so that while Mignonne and I looked if there were any more jewels, the umbrella would cover us.

It looked as if we were on the right track. There were no more jewels found. That meant that the missing jewels that the jeweller had claimed were probably from his manufacturing unit. Until we found evidence to rule out foul-play the Super had instructed us to be very discreet and careful. People from the neighbouring precinct must have observed us asking questions and if anyone was involved in this operation they could have tailed us. So, we did not spend more than five minutes. Jude, Dom and Cara pretended that they were playing a game of catch so that we could pass off as a group of kids on a regular jaunt at the beach.

Jude made a quick dash home, dropped off the umbrella and caught up with us just as we reached the Country Club. We spent only an hour there as we had a very important morning ahead of us and it was imperative that we looked the part. Cara and Mignonne had changed from their casual attire into trousers and a shirt and I had worn a formal skirt and blouse. The boys tried their best to stifle their laughter because we did not dress like this even on Sundays. However, the Super was very impressed at the way we were dressed and complimented us. The boys had to agree. The three of us could not stop smiling at their discomfiture. I had a fiendish delight picturing the two of them in formal attire with their hair swept back as they would be conducting the interviews the next day. I shared my thoughts with Cara and Mignonne and we had a good laugh.

It was a pleasant drive to the next precinct. The countryside was beautiful and there was a nice breeze blowing as we took the route along the shore that connected our two precincts. SP Jensen had a very good sense of humour and he also told us about several cases he had handled in the past. He had our rapt attention. Mignonne, who was the most attentive of all, suddenly sat upright and began scribbling something in her notebook. We asked her what it was and she brushed our question aside saying that she was just noting down some landmarks. Cara loved photography. She took several pictures of the countryside and some video clips as well. The rest of us just enjoyed the scenery and the cool sea breeze.

Cara was to conduct the first interview and Mignonne was assigned to video shoot it with the tiny hidden camera, the Super had given her. Cara and I were asked to alternate and conduct all the interviews for the day. All the employees seemed to be very honest and loyal and there did not seem to be anything suspicious about any of them. They were very polite and readily answered our questions.

It was a wonderful experience and we felt like junior reporters out to cover a very important story. The SP and the boys did not accompany us but kept a close watch on us. There was nothing untoward that took place and so ended our task for the day. Before long we were back at Dom's place where we had our lunch and reviewed the video clips and notes taken by Cara and I. The Super copied the video clips onto his iPad and Dom made a copy on his computer after which the clips were deleted from the camera.

The SP asked the boys to interview the remaining employees the following day and our little 'Gadget Princess' would once again video tape the interviews. Our plan was in place and we wondered whether we were on a wild goose chase or there would be any outcome of this exercise.

Our ever optimistic Mignonne said, "Don't despair. If we do not find the rightful owner, we can keep the jewels as a memento."

Cara said, "If you do that Mignonne, we could just as well hand you over to the Super for committing the jewel heist. It all makes sense, since it was you who found 'spectra'."

Everyone including the SP laughed. Mignonne realizing what she had unwittingly said also joined in the laughter.

All of us were invited to a birthday party that evening so we went home to rest for a while. The Super too was invited. The party was to be held in the adjoining property next to Jude's house. Our parents had excused themselves as they were exhausted after a long and gruelling week at work. Each of them had their own enterprise and this was the busiest time of the year for them.

Not just us but all the townspeople looked forward to the party as the birthday girl, Elvina's mum was an amazing cook. She was famous for her delicious finger food and fresh fruit ice-cream. We were sure that the birthday cake, too, would be yummy as she always tried out something new. Elvina, who was Mignonne's age, had a secret crush on Jude and everyone, except Jude, knew about it or at least he pretended not to know. As we were his friends, we were sure to get preferential treatment. It was an awesome party held by the poolside of their palatial villa. They even had a live band playing.

Some of Elvina's relatives lived in the neighbouring town and soon the conversation veered to the 'mystery of the missing jewels'. They were discussing it with SP Jensen. We eavesdropped but did not give ourselves away. The Super was sure to tell us all when he found an opportunity to do so.

Dinner was served and after two helpings of the amazing cake and ice-cream, we headed home. The Super dropped us home except Jude of course, as he lived next door. SP Jensen said he had a feeling that the next day would be more fruitful than today.

CHAPTER 8

We had a set routine by now, wake up, shower, go to the Country Club and then meet with the Super. As was discussed earlier, the boys would be conducting the interviews today. It was our turn to laugh at the boys because they were beyond recognition in their 'formal' clothes. SP Jensen too could not resist making a dig at them. We had built an amazing rapport with him and were very happy to spend time with our new friend, the Super. He was so simple and unassuming that often we had to remind ourselves that he was the 'Superintendent of Police'!

We took the same route as it was shorter and more pleasant. This time Mignonne had carried her field glasses and was keenly peering through them at the stretch of land along the shore. It was amazing and amusing to watch her work. She would look through the glasses and then scribble furiously in her notebook. We had been forewarned not to disturb her and since we were riding with the Super, we couldn't. The distance between our towns seemed but a trifle as we were used to the travel by now.

The boys conducted the interviews very successfully. The people they interviewed were as forthcoming as those we had spoken with the previous day and still, there was nothing shady or suspicious about anyone of them. It was half past twelve p.m. and only two employees were left on our list. It seemed as if we had come to a dead-end. Jude rang the doorbell of the last employee. A small frail looking lady came to the door. He told her he would like to interview Mr. Brown and showed her his credentials. The minute he mentioned her husband's name, the lady became very flustered and started weeping. Dom asked her to calm down. He also signalled us to join them. SP Jensen introduced himself and reassured the lady that she had nothing to fear. He requested her to let us in so that we could sit down and discuss the matter.

My pulse was racing. I could sense that we had finally made a breakthrough. I could see the excitement on everyone's faces. The lady was Mr. Brown's wife. She said she was always ill and they could barely make ends meet as they had to pay hefty bills to the doctors on account of her condition. To add to their woes, the doctor had insisted that she be operated. The cost of the surgery was beyond what they could afford. Their friends and neighbours had pooled their resources but, it was far from the amount quoted by the doctor. Mr. Brown was out all day she said, trying his best to do whatever he could to gather as many sponsors as he possibly could. To make matters worse, she said that he had come home from work last week with severe burns and had to be treated for them.

We exchanged glances but did not say a word. The Super left an envelope with money in it and wished her a speedy recovery. She invited us to come by at 4:00 p.m. that afternoon as she was certain Mr. Brown would return home by then. The Super did not want to put Mr. Brown on his guard nor alarm Mrs. Brown so he told her not to bother about the interview and that it could be conducted another day.

As soon as we left Mr. Brown's residence, SP Jensen telephoned the police officer who had accompanied us on the first day and asked him to keep a sharp lookout for Mr. Brown and tail him without arousing his suspicion.

The Super had a set expression on his face and looked very pensive so, nobody spoke a word on the way back home. I am certain all of us were bursting with curiosity but we respected the SP's silence and we knew he would certainly keep us in the loop. The case had taken a sudden turn and we seemed to be on the brink of a breakthrough.

When we reached Dom's place, the Super asked us to go home have lunch and told us he would meet us at 3:00 p.m. at Dom's. He was to head back to his police station to make a few official calls.

I knew that there was something more to the Browns' than met the eye. Mrs. Brown seemed to be far too nervous and I did not think it was just on account of her health. She had deliberately withheld the information about her husband and the illness was more of a cover up than a reality. At least that was what I thought. I wrote it down in my journal. I had my lunch, took a short nap and was at Dom's house at a quarter to 3:00 p.m. The others were already there.

SP Jensen had some important news for us. The officer had managed to tail Mr. Brown as far as the next town. He did seem to be involved in something. Of course it could be that he was collecting donations for his wife's treatment. The officer also said that Mr. Brown had a large bandage on his right hand and seemed to be in a lot of pain. We went over the roster and found out that Mr. Brown was at work on the day the missing jewels were reported. The Super told us that we would make the pending visit to the workshop the following day.

CHAPTER 9

The following day we decided against going to the Club. Instead, we met in Dom's basement to share our theories on the case. We were to leave in two hours. After we shared our views, which Mignonne recorded in the 'incognito account', we played a few indoor games.

It seemed as if slowly the bits and pieces of the puzzle were falling in place. There were a few things we still had to investigate. The Super did not want to take a chance as we did not know what we were up against. He told us we would travel in an armored car with him and the backup policemen would follow us in tourist cars. We did have some tourists at this time of the year and the policemen from our precinct, dressed in casual clothes with their cameras round their necks, did look the part.

We reached the workshop. The jeweller opened it for us. It was a large room and full of specialized tools which cost a fortune. The jeweller informed us he had employed highly skilled workers to handle each task from the time the diamonds were mined and processed up to the stage of a finished product that we saw on display in the market. Mr. Sinclair had explained how diamonds are classified and valued according to their size, shape, quality and colour. He told us there were rough diamonds of more than 16,000 categories.

He also told us how diamonds are sold at regular, invitation-only sales called "sights" to the world's leading diamond cutters, polishers and manufacturers. Sight-holders were allowed to choose to cut the rough diamonds they purchased themselves or sell some of it to smaller manufacturers and wholesalers. The next step for the rough diamond is cutting and polishing. This is a great skill, with meticulous techniques that have been practiced and perfected for generations. He quickly oriented us with the various stages a diamond or gem is processed before it reaches the market.

First, the cutter uses cleaving, sawing or laser cutting to separate the original rough diamond into smaller, more workable pieces. Then, the girdler uses a process called 'bruting' that grinds away the stone's edges and provides its outline shape. 'Faceting' follows, usually in two steps. The first 18 facets (table, culet, bezel and pavilion of a stone) are cut and polished by the blocker. The brillianteer cuts and polishes the final 40 facets, including the star, upper girdle and lower girdle. Finally, the cut gem is boiled in acids to remove dust and oil.

The polished gems are finally ready to be set into finished pieces of jewellery, which is the manufacturer's job. They are then either sold to a wholesaler, who works as a middleman to sell the manufacturer's goods, to the retailer, or sold directly to the retailer by the manufacturer. We were amazed at the number of stages a gemstone had to be processed after it was obtained from the mines and before it was presented in the market as a finished product. I was certain all this information would be significant to the case. I was curious to know more about the 'tumbling stage' and understand its working.

The jeweller told us how large quantities of roughly shaped stones are often tumbled, i.e., turned at a slow speed in a rotating barrel with abrasives and water for extended periods (days or weeks). By tumbling with progressively finer grades of abrasive (usually silicon carbide) and washing carefully between grades, the stones are gradually smoothed and polished to serendipitous but often very attractive shapes. Tumbling barrels are often hexagonal in outline in order to enhance the stirring action of barrel rotation. An alternative to rotatory tumblers is a vibratory machine, often called a vibratory tumbler, in which the containing barrel vibrates rather than rotates.

The more stationary arrangement of vibratory machines makes it much easier to examine the progress of the stones inside, whereas standard tumblers must be halted in order to check progress. In addition to polishing gemstones, tumbling is often used to polish large quantities of metal jewellery.

The jeweller informed SP Jensen that the jewels had mysteriously disappeared from the tumbling barrel on that fateful day. It was the first time in 20 years that such an incident had taken place he said. His machines were well maintained and there was no sign of corrosion. He vouched for his workers as they were all master craftsmen and very trustworthy. Besides he said, his security guards were very diligent and checked every worker when they exited from the workshop.

Their personal belongings were deposited in a different room and their uniforms did not have any pockets so, it was impossible anybody could have walked out with the jewels he added.

The Super agreed with him and we knew better as the jewels were in our possession. We had to find out who was in charge of operating the tumbling barrel that day and how the jewels had reached our stretch of the beach. The policemen who had accompanied us checked into a motel to keep up appearances of being tourists. We headed back home.

CHAPTER 10

It was exactly a week since we had found the jewels. The policemen working undercover had been tailing Mr. Brown. His movements did not seem suspicious. He was a regular visitor to the neighbouring town and he often walked down the long stretch of beach. He seemed a sort who liked his space and spent a lot of time alone. The policeman who was tailing him said he was an introvert and except for the few people he met with in the neighbouring town, there was nobody he interacted with. He seemed secretive or perhaps he was just very preoccupied with his wife's illness.

Mrs. Brown never seemed to leave the house. So, there was nothing much the policeman who was watching their house could report. As the manufacturing unit of the jewellery store was still closed, all the employees were still on leave. They were making the most of their forced holiday. The undercover policemen had stayed on and were keeping tabs on the other employees. They did not appear to be involved in the disappearance of the jewels.

Another week went by with no breakthrough in the case. We continued with our plans for the vacation and had a great time at the Country Club. Each family took turns to host parties and we had a wonderful time.

After one such occasion, Cara uploaded some pictures on our local website. I had told you how much she loved photography. It was then she came across the pictures she had taken of our trip to the next town - the beach, the countryside and the sunset. She was looking through all of them when she noticed something. She called out to Mignonne. Both of them started looking at the pictures and then Cara drew Mignonne's attention to the road adjacent to the beach. They both nodded as if the same thought dawned on them. Mignonne quickly took out her notebook and opened it to the page where she had made notes on the same day.

Yes, the same thought had struck both of them. They had observed the pipeline that ran throughout the beach and connected the fresh water supply to the three sister towns. At every intersection, there was a curve in the pipeline as a line of demarcation to each town's water supply. They had a very plausible theory as to how the jewels had landed on our part of the beach. It could be that they had managed to solve the case. Cara called the others and scheduled a meeting at Dom's tree-house.

As usual I went equipped with an assortment of sandwiches and fresh fruit drinks. My instinct told me that the ingenious duo must have some very important news for all of us.

I ran all the way to the tree-house. I could hear my heart beat and that was not because I was running but, because I was very excited. I could feel the vibes. I also knew that Cara and Mignonne had in all probability solved the mystery.

CHAPTER 11

Just as I reached the tree-house, I heard SP Jensen's voice. I was overjoyed because, the Super with his expertise in the field, would process the valuable information Cara and Mignonne were about to give us.

The Super saw me just then and called out to me, "Hey Veronica, the others are in the basement."

"Okay, Super." I yelled back, all excited and a little too loud for comfort.

I walked to the basement with the Super. Jude, Dom, Cara and Mignonne were helping Dom to set up his projector. Cara had mounted all the pictures she had taken onto slides. The curtains were drawn. The duo took over. We took our seats and listened attentively.

Cara said, "I had taken these pictures on the third day of our investigation and had forgotten all about them. Today, I was uploading some of the pictures I took at Aunt Betty's party, and I chanced upon these."

Mignonne added, "She has a very interesting theory. I believe what she says is the most plausible explanation." Mignonne looked so sincere and serious that we were in splits.

Cara gave her one of her looks and said, "Oh dear child! Do you have to make everything so dramatic?"

She looked at us and said, "Observe these slides carefully and stop me if you have any questions."

Dom had a quizzical look on his face. He looked at me and asked, "Is she giving us a test?"

"Don't be silly Dom; this is in relation to the case of the missing jewels." I said.

"But, the jewels are not missing. We found them." he replied.

Cara heard us speaking and gave us her toughest look. I had to stifle my laughter. Dom could ask the strangest of questions. He was brilliant at Math and nobody could hold a candle to his knowledge of space and spacecrafts but, he could be very silly sometimes. It never bothered him though because he was often spaced out, lost in a world of his own. I nudged him and told him to pay attention to the slide show.

We started viewing the pictures. After viewing the third slide, the Super exclaimed, "Brilliant! How did you guess? I had never thought of that angle at all."

Jude, Dom and I looked puzzled. All I had noticed in the slide show was that there was a really long stretch of water pipes in all the pictures and the beauty of the countryside. Dom was nearly asleep. Then Jude slapped his forehead, laughed out loud and started applauding.

"Well done! You two have outdone yourselves." he said.

Dom and I just shrugged our shoulders.

Dom looked at me and whispered, "What is the big deal about this slide show on water pipes? It's not as if it is about 'Rocket Science'."

I looked at him and nodded. I did not want to anger Cara again.

The Super looked at Cara and Mignonne and said, "Okay young ladies, explain away."

Cara and Mignonne had already worked out their 'presentation'. They were perfectionists and did not believe in leaving any loose ends.

Cara began with a question. She asked, "What did you notice in all the photographs?"

"Just a whole lot of water pipes." Dom replied.

"Well done Dom, you are very observant." she said.

"It's no big deal. Anyone could have made that observation. What I don't understand is why you needed to take so many pictures of the same pipes?" he said.

Cara did not take offence. We all understood Dom. He was absent-minded and harmless. I would not be surprised if he had forgotten about the jewels.

"I am zooming in on this slide. What do you observe?" Cara asked.

"Our towns get water supply through the same pipes?" I replied nervously.

"Yes, that's what it is Veronica, don't you get it? What about you Dom? Do you still find the pictures unnecessary?" she asked.

"Of course, how could I have missed it?" Dom replied.

Mignonne who had controlled herself for so long could not keep still any longer. She gave Cara an imploring look. Cara told her to be a little patient.

She then showed us the video clip she had shot. At first we did not notice anything. Then the Super asked Cara to run it again. It was then we realized that the water pipe that connected the next town seemed to be damaged at a particular spot. There was just a tiny trickle of water coming through. Most people would have missed it but, our dynamic duo had observed it when they had viewed the clip.

It was Mignonne's turn to speak. "Finally!" she said with an expression of relief. "Thank you, Cara."

"Go on child, you are trying everyone's patience." Cara said.

Mignonne looked at her in bewilderment because she had just begun to speak so she could not understand how she could be trying anyone's patience.

"Do you remember the very day Cara clicked these pictures I was writing something in my notebook?" she asked.

"Yes, you said you were noting down some landmarks." Jude replied.

"That was not what it was. I had observed the pipes and I was noting the spots where it curved and led to the next town. What Cara and I have figured out is how the jewels landed on our end of the beach." she said.

"It was not meant to land on our end but, because of the leaking water pipe when the water pressure increased, the first diamond ricocheted and escaped. The others also followed the same route but, did not land at once. There has to be a hidden pipe leading to that spot where we found the diamond. I saw a groove remember." she added.

"Yes. What I still cannot understand is how the jewels got into the pipeline in the first place?" Dom asked.

"Do you remember what the jeweller said when we visited the workshop?" SP Jensen asked.

"He had said that the jewels had disappeared mysteriously from the tumbling barrel." Dom answered.

"Yet, he maintained that the jewels had not left the room. He said his security guards were very diligent and there was no way that the employees could have made off with them. A fact we knew to be true since, the jewels are in our possession." the Super said.

"We will have to visit the Public Works Department and find out where the drain pipe from the jeweller's workshop leads." said Jude.

"That will not be a problem at all. I know the Chief Engineer very well. We were batch-mates." said SP Jensen.

"What about Mr. Brown? Is he linked to the case or not?" I asked.

"There is something that does not add up where he is concerned. All the other employees seem to be reconciled about their forced holiday except for him. Somehow, he seems restless." the Super replied.

"Perhaps we should conduct that pending interview with him." said Cara.

"Right on the button, dear. You kids are as good as professional investigators!" SP Jensen replied.

Cara turned red in the face with happiness and embarrassment. She never reacted to compliments that came her way. I, on the other hand, thrived on them. Often I would draw everyone's attention to some task I had done well and ensure that I was complimented for it.

"So, that's settled then. I will meet with my friend at the PWD today and request him to set up a field visit as research for your 'school project'. Tomorrow, I will ask Jack who is tailing Mr. Brown to assure that he is at home and inform us immediately so that, we can conduct that interview with him. It should probably be around 4:30 or 5:00 p.m." SP Jensen said.

"That's fine by us. We'll be ready to leave with you whenever you need us to." Mignonne replied. Her eyes shining with delight at the prospect.

The Super congratulated Cara and Mignonne as their amazing skills of observation had almost help solve the case. He told us to continue with our regular schedule as he did not want us to be deprived of our playtime.

We stayed at Dom's for another fifteen minutes, too excited to speak and then headed for the Country Club.

Mignonne told us on the way home that she would update the 'incognito account' and e-mail it to us from a secure connection.

True to her word, Mignonne e-mailed the update. It read as follows:

Day 1 – found 'spectra'

Day 2 – nothing to report

Day 3 – found 'spectras family members' and saw TV announcement

Day 4 – appraisal of 'spectra and family' and plans set for investigation

Day 5 – investigation begins continues till Day 7. Mr. B – check

Day 7 to Day 15 – nothing unusual to report.

Day 16 – Sister duo make some findings and call for a meeting

Day 17 – Findings discussed. PWD Engineer meeting and visit to Mr. B due.

General notes: Need to research more on tumbling barrels and water pipelines. Add your observations.

Though the e-mail seemed sketchy, we could read between the lines as we knew our dear friend Mignonne very well.

CHAPTER 12

SP Jensen called us the next morning and told us that he had met the PWD Engineer and scheduled a field visit on the following day. He told us to keep ourselves free for the day and not to schedule any matches with our neighbours. As we had discussed the previous day, we were to leave for the next town, as soon as we got the call from Jack about Mr. Brown.

I stocked my backpack with all our favourite food and there was enough to feed a small army. Dom too packed his ice-box with ice-cream and fruit juice. The temperature had risen and the summer heat was almost unbearable. There was no way we could have worn formal clothes. I doubt Mr. and Mrs. Brown would have noticed the difference. They seemed to be caught up in a web of their own.

It was almost a quarter past five when the Super got the call. We had assembled at

Dom's place at half past three to avoid any delays. It was imperative that we had that interview with the secretive Mr. Brown. We reached the town in five minutes and headed straight for their house. The Super was to conduct the interview and he asked us to keep a sharp look out for any signs. Mignonne was appointed to record the interview as she had done on the earlier occasions.

This time Mr. Brown opened the door. He was stocky in build and unlike his wife, seemed to be in the pink of health. I guess his long walks on the beach had really paid off. The Super introduced us as students who were assigned to write a paper on the 'craftsmen' of their neighbouring town. He introduced himself as our guardian and went on to explain to Mr. Brown that the school had said it was mandatory for an adult to accompany the students.

Mr. Brown stretched out his hand towards the Super and all of us observed the nasty burn he had suffered on his hand. SP Jensen pretended not to observe the burn instead he questioned Mr. Brown about his job. He told the Super that he was a 'cutter' and had been employed at the jewelers since the past two years. His father too, had been a 'cutter' as was his grandfather. SP Jensen asked him about his work hours and how he spent his weekends. He told us that he often stayed back to work at his own pace as his job was tough and it was very important that the diamond or gem-stones he cut were handled with the utmost care. Soon the SP and Mr. Brown were laughing and talking as if they had known each other for years. Mr. Brown did seem harmless but, one can never really tell right? Appearances can often be deceptive.

I was longing to ask him how he had got burnt and was just mustering up courage to do so when I heard SP Jensen ask in a very concerned tone, "Well Brown, that burn surely looks nasty, how did you get it?"

"Oh! This happened at work. I accidentally put my hand in the tumbling barrel when the acids and chemicals were in it." he answered.

All of us exchanged knowing looks except for the Super who looked at him stoically without moving a muscle. He then thanked Mr. Brown for his time and wished him a speedy recovery. We did not see Mrs. Brown so, the Super enquired about her health. Mr. Brown said that she was doing fine and was resting after 'spring cleaning' the house. I found it strange that she was doing all that work in her 'poor health condition'.

As the Super did not want to arouse any suspicion, we had travelled by my dad's car. My parents shared the same office space so; they often used only one car. So there always was one car parked in the garage.

This time we went over to my house as the Super had to drop off my dad's car. My parents had got back home from work, but were obviously tired after the day's work, so we headed for Dom's tree-house. SP Jensen was a real sport and joined us there as if he was one of us kids. It was no wonder he was the most popular person in town.

Mignonne quickly added two more points to the 'incognito account' It read as follows:

Day 18 – Visited Mr. B cause of burn seems questionable and Mrs. B seems to be faking her ill health?

The Super and all of us concurred with her findings and said both the points had to be considered very seriously.

The day had proved to be very rewarding. We had finally met the elusive Mr. Brown. He seemed to be a decent sort yet, we were almost certain, he had something to do with the disappearance of the jewels. Our 'field visit' was scheduled for the next day and perhaps a few more pieces of the puzzle would fall in place.

CHAPTER 13

At half past ten the Super met us at Dom's house. He introduced us to his friend Mr. Logan, the Chief Engineer of our town's Public Works Department. Though we had met him before, we had never interacted with him much. He was huge – almost 6 feet 7inches tall and could have carried three of us in his arms without any effort. Even, SP Jensen who was 6 feet tall looked small when compared with him. Mr. Logan was a gentle giant, very kind and loved kids so he was more than obliging to help us with our school project. We got along with him like a house on fire and it seemed more as if we were off to a picnic, with our bags full of goodies and loads of ice-cream. I almost forgot that we were part of a very important investigation.

Once again the Super drove us to the jeweller's workshop but this time he took Dom's dad's car. We were welcomed very warmly by the jeweller and he personally led us into the workshop. The manufacturing unit was still at a standstill. We headed straight to the unit where the 'tumbling barrel' was kept. The Super asked Mr. Logan to examine the barrel and tell us how the drainage system worked.

Mr. Logan wore his miner's helmet which had a powerful light attached so his hands were free to examine the barrel. Of course the barrel was empty as, the manufacturing unit was closed, so obviously, there were no chemicals in it. He focussed the beam to the drainage area. At one glance he found everything in order. Then, something caught his attention and at the same time Mignonne gave out a shrill cry and squeezed my arm. There was a dent in the tumbling barrel. It was visible only because of the light given out by the miner's helmet. Mr. Logan examined the area around the dent and found an opening in the safety net from which the jewels would have passed through without anyone's knowledge. The Super had asked his friend to keep his findings to himself so Mr. Logan did not say much. He only asked the jeweller to indicate the drainage pipe which emptied out the chemicals from the tumbling barrel.

The jeweller was not a technical man but he asked his plumber to meet us and soon the pipe was located. We walked along observing the amazing Mr. Logan at work. He reached the area where the pipe ended and made an interesting observation. The pipe seemed to have been recently repaired. He asked the plumber if he knew when it had taken place.

The man did not seem to know much but, put us on to the PWD technician in their part of the town as it was he who had ordered the repairs. He told us he'd be there in a quarter of an hour.

As it was going to be a bit of a wait, I suggested that we ate something. Everyone welcomed the suggestion. We also invited the jeweller and the plumber to join us but they declined. The Super asked the jeweller to lock the workshop as Mr. Logan had finished examining the barrel. So, he excused himself and returned to his showroom as he was expecting some clients in the next half hour or so.

After a sumptuous brunch and ice-cream, we waited patiently in the car for the PWD technician. Mr. Logan spotted him and signalled to him. He asked him why the repairs were conducted on that drainage pipe and when. The technician seemed nervous as Mr. Logan held a very high position in the

PWD and protocol demanded that he should have been consulted before any repair-work was conducted. He told the technician that such an error should never be repeated, however, he was ready to give him some consideration since he was new to the department.

The technician told Mr. Logan that the department had received several complaints about the fresh water smelling foul for the past two weeks. Many people had developed severe stomach disorders and some serious cases had even been admitted to the hospital. On investigating the water sample, they had found traces of chemicals and toxins in the drinking water. They then had begun an extensive search of all the pipelines and finally found that the drainage pipe leading out of the jeweller's workshop had been corroded. The acids and chemicals had trickled into the water source thus contaminating the drinking water. Mr. Logan was furious that he had not been informed of such a major problem. Furthermore, he was perplexed how such a thing had occurred when the drainage and fresh water pipelines ran parallel! There was no way the water could have got contaminated. He asked the technician whether the old pipes had been disposed off or whether they had been sent to the recycling unit. The technician told us that he had handed over the old pipes to the jeweller.

Once again we went back to the jeweller's shop and asked if he had preserved the corroded pipes. He did not seem very sure and we could not blame him for being absent-minded after all the problems he had faced. We waited with bated breath as the jeweller walked with us to his workshop. He took us to a smaller room and opened a cabinet. He did seem to be a very organized person for he found the corroded bits of pipe immediately and handed it over to Mr. Logan along- with a long narrow pipe. That was all that the technician had handed over to the jeweller. We realized that the waste water had entered the fresh water pipeline because it also had got corroded at the same point as the drainage pipe coming out of the jeweller's shop. How it had happened when the pipes were so far apart was the moot question?????

It was the first time ever since we had met him had we found Mr. Logan so distressed and angry. He was clearly very annoyed with the technician and we could see that it was an effort for him not to reprimand him for this major error. It was indeed a big lapse on the part of the PWD and already many of the towns-people had suffered on account of it. Mr. Logan asked the technician to carry the pipes to the trunk of Dom's dad's car.

The Super too had never seen his friend so angry. He asked him why he was reacting to this issue so violently. Mr. Logan drew his attention to the fact that it was indeed a very serious matter and it was fortunate that nobody had died on account of this carelessness. He immediately called his team from our town to report to the jeweller's shop and told them to bring all the necessary equipment. He then called the technician's superiors and fired them. He asked them to meet him in his office the following day. The 'gentle giant' really knew when to pull the reins, I thought.

The team arrived and they examined the pipe leading out of the jeweller's workshop carefully as well as the fresh water source. They found that some patchwork had been done even in the fresh water source. Though the technician had repaired the pipes, Mr. Logan asked his team to replace the drainage pipe and repair the fresh water pipe with a far superior and anti-rust pipe to avoid such an occurrence from taking place ever again and also made sure that the waste-water did not drain into any water source. He still could not figure out how that had happened in the first place as the two pipelines were far apart! We were fascinated by the thoroughness of our town's Public Works Department under the able guidance of Chief Engineer Logan. While we were making small talk, our 'Gadget Princess' Mignonne, was observing the workers very carefully. She walked up to Mr. Logan and began discussing something very seriously with him. He nodded and then turned to his men and gave them further instructions.

Our journey back home was in silence. Mr. Logan was still disturbed about the trouble the negligence on the part of the PWD had caused to the people of that town.

He looked at us and said, "This is inexcusable. Such a thing should never have taken place and certainly not on 'my watch'.

SP Jensen asked him to calm down and told him that such a thing had never occurred before. He also told him to look at the brighter side that at least the problem had been rectified in time and fortunately nobody was seriously affected. Mr. Logan said he would send a team of pathologists to conduct a series of tests on all the people of the town. He did not want anybody to have any more problems.

SP Jensen had parked his car in Dom's garage so; Mr. Logan too accompanied us to Dom's house. He apologized for losing his temper and told us never to compromise on quality control. The corrosion had taken place because the pipes had not been maintained and were sub-standard. He had sent the pipes to the PWD office to investigate the matter further.

His face suddenly lit up and he picked Mignonne up and said, "Well done little one, you are a little genius in the making! I shall inform Jensen about the report."

"I'm glad we could help. Our school teachers will be happy." she said.

As soon as the Super and Mr. Logan left, we turned to Mignonne and asked her to enlighten us about the conversation that had just taken place. She told us how she had asked the Chief Engineer to also ask the health department to check the fruits and vegetables for contamination due to the toxins in the water. She had been taught in school that disorders of the stomach could become chronic if they went unchecked. We all cheered for her and were happy to see her eyes twinkle. We were really impressed with Mignonne and Cara's brilliant methods of deduction and ability to think out of the box. The fact that they were humble and never flaunted their superior intellect made them more endearing. We waved goodbye and headed home, tired on account of the summer heat but very happy with the developments.

CHAPTER 14

Mr. Logan met SP Jensen the following day and told him that the situation in the neighbouring town was under control. He was a little less upset after he was informed by our team of doctors that the people had recovered well and all those who were admitted in the hospital too, had been discharged. The jeweller, though he had not intended to cause any discomfort to the townspeople, felt responsible for their malady. As a compensatory gesture, he offered to reimburse their hospital bills and also arranged for follow-up medication to be given to them free of cost.

This was refreshing news and we were glad to know that the towns-people were safe and out of danger. Mr. Logan had also asked his team of people to check all the water pipes leading to our town and the neighbouring towns. It would mean major repairs and that meant we needed to use up a lot of funds. Mr. Logan did not want a repeat of what had happened and told the Super that though the cost involved was steep, it was imperative that the repairs be made as soon as possible. He had suggested that all the pipes be changed and new and far superior pipes be installed. SP Jensen filled us in on the details and told us that Mr. Logan was now concerned about the funds for the repairs as it would certainly be expensive to carry them out. The Super had reassured him that we would certainly come up with a plan. After giving us the update, SP Jensen went back to the Police Station.

We were discussing the problem when Jude came up with a brilliant idea.

He said, "Remember, one of the things we had planned to do this summer was to organize an end of the holidays' party on the beach? We were to invite Elvina's parents and perhaps James' as well."

All of us started giggling the minute Jude mentioned Elvina's name. Jude just glared at us wondering what the matter was but he was too distracted with his idea to react. I almost fell on the floor laughing. I could imagine the delight on Elvina's face when Jude went over to invite her and her parents. It was adorable to see how she waited on him. The sad part was that all the attention she showered on him was lost on Jude as he was oblivious of her secret crush.

Cara was the first to regain her composure. "What do you have in mind?" she asked.

"What if we organize a week long fete for the entire town, perhaps also our two neighbouring towns instead?" he replied.

"That's a fantastic idea." we answered in unison.

"We will run it by the Super and our parents after we have planned the event to the last detail." he said.

"Yes, we will not just get to meet everyone but, we'll have loads of fun as well." I said.

"We must make it really interesting then, we'll have maximum participation and will surely collect sufficient funds in the bargain." said Cara.

"What about forming committees? We need a lot of help and it would be better if we oversee the entire event rather than try to organize it." said Jude.

"Hey! Don't get distracted! You seem to have forgotten that the case has not been solved. We have yet to establish how the jewels landed on the beach." said Dom.

"Sure, pal. You are absolutely right. I only came up with this idea to help ease the pressure of the imminent cost of repairing the water pipeline." answered Jude.

"I'm sure the Super and Mr. Logan will love your plan." said Mignonne in all sincerity.

All of us fell on the floor laughing. Our little Mignonne took on every task as if her life depended on it.

"We'll see. Let's get started on the requirements. Then the next step would be to form the committees." said Jude.

I was wonderstruck as were the others, at the level of detailing Jude was capable of. In precisely an hour, he had short-listed heads for all the committees – the caterer, the sponsors, the talent competitions, the game stalls, and the magazine committee (meant to showcase the literary skills of the children of the town). He had also thought of organizing a raffle way before the event. He said that it would cover the cost of the infrastructure and we would have a working capital. I was certain the Super and Mr. Logan would be more than happy with Jude's idea.

The Super and Mr. Logan met us in the evening at the Country Club. They had come to play a game of squash. Jude told the Super we wished to discuss something important. He told him they would meet us at Dom's house at 7:00 p.m. Jude invited him to dine at his home, but SP Jensen said he had plans. We too played for a while then, after an hour, we left for our homes to shower and were back at Dom's house in 20 minutes.

Jude arrived a little later. He had managed to put together a power point presentation. The Super and Mr. Logan loved the idea of the fete and only requested us to run it by our parents as well. They were thrilled with the plan. So were we.

CHAPTER 15

There was a lot to organize and we had to have several meetings with the different committees. The event had to be discussed with the Mayor of our towns. We had a common Mayor as the three towns were sister towns, only demarcated by the indent of the land leading to each one of them. The towns were connected by a common shoreline. The Mayor suggested that we hold the fete on the beach as it was easily accessible and equidistant to the residents of our three towns. He also gave us names and telephone numbers of people who would be able to assist us put the event together from the other two towns. By doing that he said, they too would be involved and it would assure us better footfalls at the fete. The Mayor was kind enough to offer to attend all the meetings and lend his support to ensure that the event was a success.

The Super and Mr. Logan visited us almost every day. A couple of days went by in this manner with us meeting with the various committees and monitoring the progress of each. At the end of every day, we would assemble at Dom's place to review and document all that had been completed. Our parents were very supportive and happy that we were involved in such a noble cause.

At the end of one such day, we were relaxing at Dom's as usual, taking stock of all that we had achieved so far and munching on the delicious sandwiches my mum had made when suddenly, Mignonne tugged really hard at my sleeve.

"What is it? Speak up girl." said Cara.

Cara could sense that Mignonne had thought of something really important.

"Hey! Do you remember the injury Mr. Brown had suffered? Didn't he say he had got burnt when he accidentally put his hand in the tumbling barrel when there were chemicals and acids in it?" she asked.

"Yes I remember. What is the connection?" I asked.

"Well! He had no business near the tumbling barrel at all!" she said.

"How do you know that Mignonne?" asked Cara.

"That is because Mr. Brown is a 'cutter' and does not need to be in that section of the manufacturing unit at all." she replied.

"How did none of the other employees tell us about Mr. Brown's accident?" said Cara.

"Come to think of it, I don't remember the jeweller speaking about the accident either." I said.

"I think we must ask the Super to pay Mr. Brown another visit." said Jude.

"Yes 'Princess' you've done it again." I said and gave Mignonne a tight hug.

"Great deduction, sport!" said Dom.

"Well done, sis!" said Cara.

"You don't miss a thing! Brilliant work, kiddo." said Jude.

"Thank you. Thank you very much." said Mignonne doing her imitation of the 'King' himself.

Jude told us he would get in touch with the Super and Mr. Logan and give them an update on what we had just discussed. I told him it was better if he gave them the information in person because, if by some strange chance there was a cross connection in the phone lines, someone would overhear the conversation. Jude laughed and assured me that he would meet the Super and give him the information in person. I was always teased by my friends of being extra-cautious. I truly believed in the adage 'better safe than sorry'.

As we had nothing more to discuss, we left for our homes. I was eager to know what the SP and Mr. Logan had to say about Mignonne's theory. I had a very strong feeling we would soon solve the case.

CHAPTER 16

The following morning at precisely 6:00 a.m. Cara sent us an update on the case from the incognito account. It read as follows:

Hi,

I would like you to go over the points mentioned and let us know if you have any further thoughts regarding the case. Please delete the mail from your inbox once you have read it.

We have established the following so far:

The jewels belong to the jeweller and are authentic.

The jewels landed on our end of the beach through the fresh water pipe line via the drainage pipe leading out of the jeweller's shop. This was due to the corrosion that was caused by the chemicals and acids emitted out of the tumbling barrel. The acids had managed to corrode the water pipeline adjacent to the drainage pipe and the waste water had thus entered the fresh water pipeline.

The jewels had entered the source of fresh water via the same route as the waste water which had contaminated it.

The jewels had ricocheted on account of the leak in the fresh water pipeline leading to our town. This took place when the pressure in the water pipeline had increased.

Mr. Brown had no business near the 'tumbling barrel' as he was employed as a 'cutter'.

We have yet to gather evidence and establish the following:

Mr. Brown's involvement in the disappearance of the jewels.

The seriousness of Mrs. Brown's illness which points us to a plausible motive for Mr. Brown's involvement in the case.

The role of the narrow pipe found by the technician near the fresh water pipeline.

The entry point of the jewels from the jeweller's drain into the fresh water pipeline as they ran parallel and there was no way the water from the drain could have got into the fresh water pipeline.

The fresh water outlet from where the jewels had landed on our side of the beach.

Let us meet at Dom's by 9:00 a.m. and then go ahead with our plans for the fete. Jude can tell us about his meeting with the Super and Mr. Logan. Once this is sorted out, we can go ahead with our plans for the day.

See you soon,

Cara.

I read the e-mail and promptly deleted it. Cara had covered all the details of the case so far. Mr. Brown did seem involved in the case. However, I somehow did not feel we quite knew the truth about Mrs. Brown. I mentioned this when we met at Dom's at 9:00 a.m.

"I feel Mrs. Brown is faking her illness." I said.

"What makes you say that, Veronica?" Dom asked me.

"When we met her, no doubt she looked frail and ill but, could it be that she too, like the other people of the town, was down with a severe stomach infection caused by the contaminated water?" I asked.

"Yes, in all probability yes!" yelled Mignonne in excitement.

"Why did she tell us about the donations and the operation then? Did she not think we could check these facts?" Cara asked.

"Yes. She had us totally convinced. Even the Super got taken in by her story. Remember, he even gave her money in an envelope?" said Jude.

"She must have known that we would respect her privacy and to spare her the embarrassment of her illness, we would not discuss it with others." I said.

"She seems to be a crafty woman." Cara said.

"There has to be a reason though." said Dom.

"Well! Mr. Brown works in a jeweller's manufacturing unit and he handles jewels worth millions! That in itself is enough reason for a person with no scruples." said Cara.

"I somehow cannot picture Mr. Brown doing that." said Jude.

"He may not want to but, his wife may compel him to. There is more to them than meets the eye. We will have to subtly ask the neighbours about them." I said.

"I am meeting the Super at 10:00 a.m. in the Country Club. I'll tell him all that we have just discussed. In all probability he may ask us to accompany him to visit Mr. and Mrs. Brown, today." said Jude.

"Do we all need to do that? I have two meetings scheduled for the morning – one with the Catering committee and the other with the decorators." I said.

"That makes sense. Cara and Mignonne, you accompany the Super. Dom, Veronica and I will stay back and go ahead with our earlier plans for the day." Jude said.

"We did not make any plans for the day. This will suit us fine." said Cara.

"Okay then, we'll meet at Dom's at 6:00 p.m." said Jude.

Cara and Mignonne accompanied Jude for his meeting with the Super. They set off for the neighbouring town at half past 10 a.m. I quickly packed a huge bag of goodies for Cara, Mignonne and the Super. We saw them drive off in the Super's car. Then Jude, Dom and I went to attend our meetings.

The committees had done their homework very well and I was very happy with the way the plans for the fete were coming along. We had just a week left to put everything in order. The fete was being held on 'Founders' Day' as a memorial to our great grandfathers who had built these beautiful and peaceful towns. You may recall me mentioning that the festivities would last for a week.

All through the day, I wondered how much personal information Cara, Mignonne and the Super had managed to glean out of Mr. and Mrs. Brown. I could have totally misjudged Mrs. Brown for all I know. I told myself to be patient and that all would be revealed by 6:00 p.m. Time seemed to be at a standstill, I had nothing more to do so, I baked some tea-cakes and made some fresh fruit juice. How I wished I had accompanied them!

The Super, Cara and Mignonne arrived a little after 6:00 p.m. Their visit was enlightening and the trio said there was no doubt that Mr. and Mrs. Brown were hiding some information. Cara's suspicion that Mrs. Brown was perhaps the one calling the shots seemed to be right. This was the first time the couple had been present in the same room at the same time. Mignonne told us that though she did not tell Mr. Brown off, Mrs. Brown was able to silence him with one look.

The Super had instructed the undercover officer to watch them very closely and also sent him two more officers as backup. He told us he would check the hospital records to see if Mrs. Brown did have a problem or was faking it. Cara had also suggested that Mr. Brown's GP be questioned regarding his burn. The Super said it would not be a problem getting it checked out as he knew the dean of the hospital really well as he did the town GP.

All of us were exhausted that day so we went home. We had more than enough to occupy our thoughts and we had a packed schedule ahead till the fete.

CHAPTER 17

I was going over all that Cara, Mignonne and the Super had said the previous day about Mr. and Mrs. Brown. SP Jensen told us that he would make the inquiries on his own as he did not want to upset our schedule and told us he would meet us at a half past six in the evening at Jude's house.

Each of us had meetings with different committees and the decorators too had been asked to come to the beach to set up their equipment and start with the lay out for the fete. We had a nice, wide sandy beach and it could easily accommodate a floating crowd of over a thousand people. There was access through the long stretch of concrete road and as there would be several entry and exit points, there would be no crowding. The food-court was going to be a huge covered area with several counters of delicious cuisine from all over the globe. Our towns did boast of the best chefs in the world.

We met at my home for lunch. I loved to cook and was glad my friends enjoyed the food I cooked. Of course, my cooking could not be compared to the fancy gourmet food Cara turned out. She was an amazing cook and the way she presented the meal made it all the more appetising. We were done with our meetings for the day and had to go over to Jude's home at half past six to meet the Super. It was just 3:00 in the afternoon so; we played a game of monopoly which Jude obviously won.

We went over the points Cara had e-mailed us. If there was one thing we could check on our own, it would be the fresh water outlet from where the jewels had landed on the beach. Mignonne had a 'theory' so she told us that she would once again like to check the spot where we had found 'spectra'. As we had done so on the previous occasion, we went equipped with Jude's beach umbrella, spades and pails to make sand castles. We had agreed that Mignonne and I would check the area where the jewels were found and the others would build sand castles. To an onlooker, it would seem like we were just a bunch of children having a good time playing on the beach.

The boys set up the beach umbrella and began building sand castles. Mignonne started digging around the area where she had found the jewels. After ten minutes, she managed to uncover a drainpipe that was hidden under the sand.

"How foolish I've been. We have practically lived on this beach every summer holiday and yet I missed such an important detail." she said.

"What detail?" I asked.

"Let's join the others and discuss this later." she replied.

Dom, Jude and Cara had made such an amazing castle that I had to click a picture of it. It also gave me an idea for the fete. I thought we could also include this – designing sand castles, as one of our competitions. We could post the images of the winners on our local website. It was half past four and our pails and footwear were very sandy. We were strictly instructed by our parents not to carry the sand into the house. We quickly washed ourselves and the pails in the washroom built especially for the kids who came to play on the beach. We were heading back to our homes when it struck us. It was almost like a lightning bolt.

"Of course, it has to be." said Cara.

"How could we have forgotten?" said Jude.

"At times one does tend to forget something which is obvious as it has always been there." I said.

"Three cheers for Mignonne! You've done it once again." said Dom.

I was not too sure if Dom had any clue of what was happening but, he seemed overjoyed as well. This was an amazing find and we now knew how the jewels had landed on our stretch of the beach. We had tied this end of the case and if all went well, the Super would have gathered concrete evidence on Mr. and Mrs. Brown.

We were at Jude's home when the Super called and said he would not be meeting us as he had a few more things to clear up and he did not want to leave it for another day. He asked us to go ahead with our plans and said he would meet us the next day at 9:00 a.m. at Jude's house.

Cara and Mignonne said they would update the incognito account with the latest findings. I told them that I had to head back home as I had offered to help my mom to make jelly sweets and jam. She was the head of the committee in charge of the prizes for the hoopla game. There was a lot to be achieved in six days and since the Super was not meeting us the others decided to use the time at hand to review the targets for the fete.

I received a message on my cell phone from Cara late in the night telling me that the committees were doing really well and that she was positive the fete would be a grand success.

CHAPTER 18

The next morning, I logged into my e-mail account and found that Cara had not posted anything. I showered, dressed and packed my backpack with all the possible goodies. I also packed a few jelly sweets for my friends. They loved the confectionery my mom made.

We were to meet at Jude's house. I was early but the others arrived soon after me. It was just 8:00 a.m. so obviously the discussion veered towards the previous day's findings.

Jude asked us to go over the earlier week's findings when we had visited the jeweller's shop with the Super and Mr. Logan. He told us to recall how after examining the tumbling barrel, Mr. Logan had pointed out a dent and an opening wide enough for the jewels to escape. Mr. Logan and his team had further established that the waste water from the jeweller's shop had entered the pipeline that carried the drinking water. We deduced that the diamonds and other jewels had also entered the water source in the same manner.

Jude then drew our attention to how Mignonne had found 'spectra' in a groove. As we had not wanted to arouse suspicion, we had gone to the beach only twice after the first day of our holidays. We had not been able to investigate the matter further. Then yesterday, Mignonne had asked us to go back to that area of the beach and when she dug up the spot where she found 'spectra' she unearthed a drainpipe. All that was left for us to do after that was to ascertain which fresh water pipeline it led out of.

All of us knew the beach like the back of our hands. We knew everybody and were friends with everyone. Our houses were the closest to this particular stretch of the beach. Our parents had built a neat washroom for us so that we would not carry the sand back into the house. They had employed old Mr. Jackson to maintain the place. He was short-sighted but kept the place sparkling clean. He adored us and knowing that our summer holidays were beginning soon, he must have cleaned the washroom. On account of the sand, and his eyesight, he must have missed seeing the jewels gushing out of the water pipe. In all probability he had taken off the safety net so that the sand would flow down the drain when he washed the restroom. That was how the jewels had come to rest where they did — out of the washroom drain and into the drainpipe in which 'spectra' got embedded in the groove and sand preventing the other jewels from also spilling out.

Of course, later, the other jewels had come to settle in the box that Mignonne had left behind once we used the washroom. Dom was the first to react after Jude finished speaking.

"It was as simple as that! Yet, it did not seem so at first." he said. We could not control our laughter.

"Glad we are on the same wavelength, buddy." said Jude.

"I most certainly am! What do you take me for, pal?" he asked Jude with a quizzical look on his face.

I was not sure if Dom was on the same page as us, since, our deduction about the jewels, did not pertain to 'space' or 'rocket science'. However, if any of us had any queries on the 'said subject', Dom was our walking and talking encyclopedia. Also, though he was absent-minded, he was a real sport. He also had the most expensive and latest equipment that he was more than glad to share with all of us. He was an only child but he did not have a single selfish bone in his body.

I pulled out the jelly sweets and was distributing them when the Super arrived. Jude gave him the gist of our discussion and he too agreed that our deduction was totally plausible. He told us to be absolutely sure; we could have it checked out by pouring some other similar sized objects down the drain. Cara who could not contain her curiosity any more, asked SP Jensen about Mr. and Mrs. Brown.

What SP Jensen had to narrate to us had us totally stupefied!

CHAPTER 19

The Super told us that he had gone unannounced to the Brown's residence. His officers too, did not know he was going to visit them. As he approached closer he could see a silhouette of a person behind the curtains of the upstairs window. He rang the doorbell. The person concerned seemed to be taking his or her time to answer the door. After waiting for five minutes in this fashion, the SP had stepped back only to notice that the person had not moved from the window. He found it very strange!

There did not seem to be any movement or activity of any kind from within the house. He called out to Mr. Brown and knocked on the door, still there was no answer. The person at the window too, had not moved a muscle. Once again, the Super tried to draw that person's attention, to no avail. SP Jensen realized that something was terribly wrong. He paged his friends from that precinct to meet him at the Brown's residence immediately. The undercover policemen who had been watching the house had already arrived as soon as they saw the Super go to the residence.

SP Jensen's friends arrived. Together, they broke open the door. There did not seem to be any sign of anyone in the house. They fanned out and began searching the house. The officers from our precinct were instructed by the Super to guard the door. SP Jensen and an officer went upstairs to check on the person who was sitting by the window.

The door leading to the room was locked from the inside so; they once again had to break open the door. The sight they saw was enough to make anyone's blood run cold and send shivers down their spine. Mr. Brown was lying on the bed in a pool of blood! The Super checked and found there was a faint pulse. He called for the paramedics who also confirmed that Mr. Brown was alive. They carried him downstairs and admitted him to the hospital where an emergency operation had to be conducted. The Surgeon had found a deep gash across Mr. Brown's stomach and told the SP that it was a miracle that none of the other internal organs had been damaged. It was a major surgery and would take him a long time to recover. Mr. Brown had not regained consciousness after his surgery and was still not out of danger.

The silhouette was not that of Mrs. Brown. It was a life-size cardboard cutout which had been propped against the window to make it seem as if there was someone seated at the window. Mrs. Brown was not in the house. The officers had searched the premises thoroughly. She had disappeared into thin air! How she had managed to do that with the officers watching the house so diligently was very surprising. The Super instructed the officers to dust the house for fingerprints and look for the knife used to attack Mr. Brown. There was no sign of any struggle on his part so; it seemed as if he was asleep when he was attacked.

SP Jensen told us that Mrs. Brown had escaped without a trace. The officers were instructed by him to keep looking for her. He also had her picture posted in the missing person's list in our local newspaper and e-mailed to the neighbouring towns. She seemed to have set out on foot as she had not taken the car which was still in the garage.

This was sensational news indeed! We had never in our wildest dreams thought the case would take such a turn!

The Super told us that he would rather we did not accompany him anymore. It was certainly a case of attempted murder. If he had not gone that morning to check on Mr. and Mrs. Brown, Mr. Brown would have succumbed to his injuries. The surveillance team was still on the lookout for Mrs. Brown and the Homicide team had been roped in to give their expert opinion.

I could not understand why Mrs. Brown had cut open her husband's stomach – if she was the killer, when she could have easily smothered him with a pillow? Nobody would have suspected her and she could have claimed that he asphyxiated in his sleep. I was lost in my own theory about the case when I realized that the Super was speaking with me.

I had this terrible habit, once I got thinking about something, I would get so involved that I would forget where I was. My friends knew how I was and would tease me about it. Jude and Dom often pretended to have shared some very important information when I was lost in a reverie. Before we became really good friends, I often was fooled by them and would sulk at not being given that information however, now I knew better so their friendly banter did not affect me at all and I played along.

"I beg your pardon sir, I was deep in thought." I said.

"That is precisely what I said, young lady — a penny for your thoughts. I guess I'll have to bid higher as you seem to have thought of something very important." said the Super with a broad grin on his face.

"Yes sir, I was wondering why the killer went for Mr. Brown's stomach when she could have easily smothered him with a pillow. It would have seemed like an accident and nobody would have suspected her." I said.

"That's a very good observation, dear girl! I had not thought of that angle at all! You kids are brilliant!" SP Jensen said looking at me in amazement.

"Could it be that she wanted to frighten him and did not intend to attempt to kill him?" Dom asked.

"I presume he may have been asleep as there did not seem to be any sign of a struggle. Besides, Mr. Brown is certainly stronger than Mrs. Brown." answered the Super.

"Perhaps she had an accomplice?" Dom said.

"Yes, we need to check that out. What beats me is the fact that we have not been able to trace her yet, considering she has escaped on foot. I have asked my men to keep a sharp lookout for her. She may still be in the area." The Super said.

"Then Mr. Brown is still in danger." Cara said.

"Yes. He is a threat to the killer if he recovers. The doctors are monitoring him very carefully and my friends in the precinct are keeping guard round the clock. I have also strictly banned visitors. As he is in the I.C.U. we can do the needful without seeming obvious." SP Jensen said.

"Have you posted a guard at the jeweller's shop?" asked Mignonne.

"No. I haven't. The jeweller has a very diligent security force. They are very loyal and thorough. Why did you want me to post a guard, dear?" the Super asked Mignonne.

"I feel Mrs. Brown may try to visit the jeweller at his shop." she answered.

"I don't think the jeweller will attend to her as she is not a client. The workshop is closed so, she has no business there." The Super reassured her.

"I think I know what Mignonne's trying to tell us. She fears for the jeweller's safety. In fact sir, it would be better if you have policemen posted outside his shop and his home." Cara said.

"I will have to do that very subtly. I do not want to unnerve the jeweller nor arouse his suspicion." SP Jensen said.

We nodded our heads in agreement.

"Have you ever handled a situation like this in your career so far? At least I do not recall any crime taking place in our town." Jude asked.

"I have trained for this and I was posted in a city for five years. So, I have dealt with worse crimes than this. It has been very peaceful in our town though." The Super replied.

"The fete begins in two days. We've got to have enough security even then. There is a lot of money involved." said Jude.

"The money will be handled by your parents and Dom's dad will be the custodian to keep the money in his safe till we hand it over to Mr. Logan. I have worked out a plan with them already." The Super said.

"At least we are aware and can take the necessary precautions." said Dom.

"That's right. We have a very secure and centralized area from where the people can collect their food coupons and game coupons. The exit is also very secure and we have cordoned off an area which will lead into Dom's house. There is a façade being created that will camouflage the exit. Only your parents, you and my team of officers know about this." SP Jensen said.

"As we are overseeing the event, we do not have any specific duties. We will be at the 'Helpline tower' to handle any emergency. Mr. Logan and two of his men will be with us." said Jude.

"You have thought of everything kids! Have you organized such events before?" The Super asked in wonderment.

"We have not had an opportunity to do so before but, we have picked up these skills by observing our teachers at school and when we've gone out camping." I said.

"Wow! You are excellent students. Everyday I learn something more from you." said the Super.

"Jude is the one who thinks everything through till the last detail and we just follow what he has to say." said Mignonne.

"It is wonderful how you have identified your strengths and are utilizing it to benefit everyone." SP Jensen said.

"It is a pity though that Jude's siblings and my sister are missing all the fun." I said.

"Oh yes! Megan, Karl and Jodie are at camp. I had forgotten all about them. When will they be back?" asked the Super.

"In two weeks." I replied.

"I'm sure they're having a great time at camp." SP Jensen said.

"None of their activities in camp can measure up to what we've been part of this summer!" said Jude.

"We did plan loads of fun things for the summer holidays but, never did we dream of it turning out the way it has." said Cara.

"A pity about Mr. Brown though! I really hope he survives." I said.

"We can pray for him." The Super replied.

CHAPTER 20

The day of the fete arrived. We had a dry run the day before. Everything had been thought out to the last detail by Jude and had been converted by the committees. There was a lot of excitement in the air. Since it was 'Founders' Day' we were to begin the fete with a small memorial service followed by a song by the five of us. Besides our other interests, we also had our own little 'band'.

The service was to begin at 9:00 a.m. The Super had asked us to meet him at Dom's house before the service. He wanted us to arrive at the venue at the same time and felicitate us for all that we had done for the town. Jude told him we did not need any recognition and that we had done all we had out of our loyalty and love for our town and its people. The Super had insisted on going ahead with his plan as he wanted to inspire the youth in our town by citing our example. We were very excited and our only prayer was that everything should go according to plan. You could have heard us breathe, we were that silent!

Without warning, Mignonne suddenly shouted out, "What if she is disguised?"

"Whom are you referring to?" we asked.

"Mrs. Brown. She could have disguised herself. That is why the officers did not see her leave. They were looking for a frail and petite lady. I think she is still around and in disguise." she answered.

"That is possible. I will instruct my men to look out for strangers. We do not have any tourists visiting at this moment. I shall also tighten the security at the hospital. Good thinking little one." SP Jensen said.

The Super immediately got in touch with his department and doubled the security at the coupon counter and at the hospital. Mr. Brown had not yet gained consciousness. He was still in the Intensive Care Unit. SP Jensen had also instructed his men not to permit *anyone*, even his *wife* to visit him.

The 'Founders' Day' memorial ceremony was conducted very beautifully by our Vicar. The beach was packed with the people of all the three towns. Then it was our turn to perform. Cara had written the lyrics, the boys composed the melody and Mignonne and I were the lead singers. It was a song about our wonderful town and all the beautiful people in it. The lyrics were passed around and we managed to get all the people to sing along the second time. The kids of all the three towns had put together a spectacular dance/drama depicting what our towns stood for. The senior citizens of all the three towns were felicitated. The fete was then declared officially open by the Mayor.

The response was beyond our expectations. We were already halfway to achieving our target with the first day's collection alone. As 'Founders' Day' was a public holiday the people of all the three towns had participated enthusiastically and spent a lot of money. We were positive we would have the same response at the weekend. There were interesting events lined up for the weekend which had been publicised via our local website. We were certain we would achieve our target as we already had hundreds of inquiries and enrollments for the various competitions. Jude had managed to get sponsors for every event so the prizes too were taken care of. It was thanks to his incredible foresight and people-skills that we would not have to settle any dues after the event. This was perhaps the first time that after an event of such a magnitude the net profit would be equal to the gross profit. Jude was already a financial wizard at the age of fifteen!

Dom's dad was in charge of the money collected at the fete and had deposited it in the massive safe in his house. As the access to his house was cordoned off there was no way anybody could enter his home without permission. His house was almost like a fortress and we felt very important as we were among the select few who were permitted entry to his home. Dom called it his spacecraft. In fact, the façade was made to look like a spaceship. There was an official photographer to click people's photographs against the façade if they wanted to.

The kids of all the three towns were having the time of their lives. There were several competitions for the parents to take part in as well. At any given time of the day we had a crowd of at least five hundred. This was the first time, we had organized something of this magnitude involving the three sister towns. We were really glad with the way things had turned out.

Mr. Logan and his men kept us in splits with their friendly banter. I don't think I'd eaten so much in my life as I did during the fete. As we were the VIPs we were sent samples of food at regular intervals so we got to taste cuisine from all parts of the globe throughout the day. We knew we would have to exercise vigorously to get rid of the extra weight we'd all gather on account of the delicious food we had tucked in everyday of the fete.

Every evening there was something really special planned. This evening there was a hip hop group dance competition both for the children and their parents. We had twenty five groups participating and were sure it would be very enjoyable. If anybody was not keen on watching the dance, they were free to spend time at the games stalls. Everyone had something to interest them or entertain them. There were tattoo artists, caricature artists, face painting artists, nail artists, and sketch artists to name a few. There was never a dull moment and it was very fulfilling to see everyone so happy.

There was still no sign of Mrs. Brown and it was already the second day of the fete. The policemen were very diligent and it was impossible for a stranger to enter the premises. The officers under the expert supervision of SP Jensen were given relief and worked in shifts, so they were alert and not overburdened. There was a surveillance system set up and the cameras were positioned such that it was impossible for the officers to miss a thing.

The challenge would be during the weekend. It would also be the last two days of the fete and we were expecting a bigger crowd. Many of the patrons had invited their relatives from out of town for the fete. The entrances to the venue were from different points though the coupon counter was just one. It was impossible for the Super to be in ten places at the same time. He did not want us to be around either as he feared for our safety. He told us not to leave the 'Helpline tower' nor attend to anyone on our own. Mr. Logan and his subordinates were huge and could take on an army. SP Jensen had briefed him about the danger involved after Mr. Brown's attempted murder.

SP Jensen told us that he had still had not informed anybody about the jewels that had been found. He however had informed his superior in the city whom he had worked under. The CP had also advised him to hold on to the jewels and asked him to inform him if he needed any help.

The jeweller had to be protected as he was an elderly man and would never suspect a person as frail and helpless looking as Mrs. Brown. The Super had doubled the security at his house and the guards at his shop had been instructed not to permit anyone into the shop or the house. The shop was not easily accessible and there were enough surveillance cameras and bullet proof doors and alarms installed. It was obvious that a place like that had to be well guarded. The Super told us that one could never be too careful and it was better to have the extra security to avoid innocent people getting hurt. I whole heartedly agreed with him. My friends always teased me as being overcautious so they had a good laugh at my expense. I told them later, I was justified in behaving in such a manner and I was happy I had an ally in SP Jensen who thought the same.

CHAPTER 21

Mr. Brown was getting better and was out of danger. He had regained consciousness but, was still not coherent of his condition or his surroundings. He had suffered a serious injury and had to be heavily medicated to deal with the pain. The Super did not want to add to his stress so; he had not yet questioned him about the attack. The officers guarding him reported to the Super that surprisingly, Mr. Brown had not asked to see his wife even once. That was strange as she was his only relative! His parents were orphans and had passed away many years ago and he was their only child.

The Super made it a point to check on him thrice everyday. The doctors attending to him told SP Jensen that it would be a while before Mr. Brown could move out and get on with his work. The Super had arranged for a nurse to look after him in a nursing home in our town, once he was discharged. The doctors said it would be at least a week to ten days before that would happen.

The weekend celebrations were well underway and as we had anticipated, the crowd was double that of 'Founders' Day'. The committees were well aware of this and had extra hands to help them manage their stalls more efficiently. Jude had chosen the heads of each committee so well that not once we were bothered with queries or glitches. They were brilliant, each and every one of them, and it did not seem as if they were first timers at all. In fact, to an onlooker, it seemed as though organizing fetes and events was a regular feature with them.

At the 'Helpline tower' all we had to do was keep a lookout for anyone who needed help or manpower. This was the sixth day of the fete and everything was going on as planned. We were virtually at a loose end as the committees

were well equipped and there was not a thing for us to do. Each of us was watching the progress of the fete on the monitors set up in the 'Helpline tower' so, we did not actually miss any of the fun. It was also made us feel good to think that we were in a way responsible for so many people having a good time.

I was seated beside Cara and we were munching on an amazing almond macaroon baked by Elvina's mom. Mr. Logan was chatting with the boys and Mignonne was eating a chocolate donut, her favourite. Cara was merrily humming a tune when something caught her attention.

"I did not know of Mrs. Jonas' twin sister." she said.

"She does not have a twin sister." I replied.

Mrs. Jonas was a lovely lady who had two married daughters living in New York. She was always happy to meet us and often helped at the 'Country Club'. Our families had known her for years. She was very active though over the years, she had really piled on the pounds. It was due to a thyroid condition, she had explained. There was never an occasion that took place without Mrs. Jonas taking centre stage. She could put a smile on the face of the grouchiest person. She was entertaining as well as one of the kindest people we knew. All the children of our town loved to visit her as she always had treats and goodies saved for all of us.

"Of course she does, look!" said Cara.

"I know she does not have a twin sister, but, that lady does look a lot like Mrs. Jonas." Mignonne said.

"I'll ask Jensen to get someone to talk to her right away." said Mr. Logan.

"You'll have to ask the Super to get hold of both the sisters and take them to separate places for questioning. I have a feeling that something's not quite right." said Mignonne.

"Yes, we've known the Jonas family for years and as far as I know, she has never mentioned a twin sister." I said.

We exchanged knowing looks and all had the same thought running through our minds, we may have just found the elusive Mrs. Brown. The Super managed to detain both the ladies separately by telling them they had won a prize on their purchase of coupons. There were many empty cubicles for people to rest when they were tired. SP Jensen posted his officers outside each of the cubicles and went inside to question one of them. She was without doubt the Mrs. Jonas that we all knew of. The Super gave her the 'prize' she had supposedly won, congratulated her and saw her off. He then went to the second cubicle where Mrs. Jonas' twin was seated. As soon as she saw the Super, she let out a cry and fainted. SP Jensen was already prepared for something dramatic so, he did not fall for her ploy. He had also consciously left his weapons with his subordinate officers. He did not want any unnecessary scuffle to take place. He let the 'twin' fall to the ground and waited. She did not stir. He quickly filled a glass of water from the water-cooler installed in the cubicle and threw it on this Mrs. Jonas' face.

She got up and looked around as if in a daze and pretended to be lost. The Super blew his whistle and a female constable from our precinct entered the cubicle. Then, on the Super's behest, she deftly peeled off the mask covering Mrs. Jonas' twin's face. It was Mrs. Brown alright! She had managed to wear a mask to make her look like the original Mrs. Jonas. She had worn a fat body suit so; everyone who met her identified her as Mrs. Jonas. The officers too, had not suspected that she was not the original Mrs. Jonas.

The lady constable quietly led Mrs. Brown away through a less crowded route. The Super and two more officers accompanied them. We could see every bit of the action from the 'Helpline tower'. The entire 'operation' was conducted so swiftly that except for us, nobody realized that anything was amiss. There were several inter-town matches organized to make the fete more interesting. There was a huge electronic score board which displayed the scores of each town. At that moment everyone was watching the semi-final volleyball match between our town and the third sister town.

The winner of this match would play against the second town. Each town had one chance to redeem themselves. The third sister town already lost to the second town. They were however, putting up a good fight to get back in the league. The spectators from each town were cheering for their teams. It was an amazing match and it took all the skill our players possessed to win the match. The finals were to be held the next day – the last day of the fete. This was the last match of the day. After tallying the scores of the various events and this match, the score board showed our town leading by 50 points. The second and third sister towns were neck to neck. The 50 point lead could be covered easily by the second town if, they won the volley ball match. Then they would be awarded the 'Championship Cup'.

SP Jensen had to arrest Mrs. Brown as the lead suspect in the attempted murder of Mr. Brown. It was certainly a non-bailable offense. The SP had read her rights to her which stated that she was permitted to make a phone call to her lawyer and would be appointed one if she had none. She said she did not have a lawyer so, the Super arranged for a lawyer for her. Miss Simone the lawyer was a champion of the weak and downtrodden and would surely fight

Mrs. Brown's case to give her a fair trial. The Super had asked the lady constable to search Mrs. Brown's person thoroughly so that she would not attempt to escape. The fingerprint expert had sent her prints to the CP from the city - SP Jensen's friend who would check their database for any past offenses committed by her. He said as it was already Saturday, we would get the results only on Monday.

The Super had confined Mrs. Brown in a maximum security cell which was impossible to break out of. It was SP Jensen's first arrest ever since he was assigned to head the police department of our precinct. As our three towns were sister towns, SP Jensen had the jurisdiction to arrest her.

As it was a Saturday, it was almost eleven p.m. by the time we wound up the day's events. The special event for that evening, an 'on the spot' talent competition had three hundred and fifteen participants. We were really thrilled with the response. As was our regular practice now, we met with the Super in Dom's basement. The money had to be counted and records maintained. Mr. Logan also accompanied us.

Dom's dad and my dad counted the money on an hourly basis so that it was easier for them at the end of the day. Mr. Logan also joined them in Dom's dad's study where they were counting the last hour's collection. While we were waiting for them in the basement, the Super quickly informed us about Mrs. Brown. He told us that they had given her a sedative so that she would not attempt anything untoward. We marvelled at her ingenuity at disguising herself. That is how she had given the slip to the officers watching the house. Mrs. Jonas regularly visited her friends from the next town. Mrs. Brown knew nobody would suspect her if she was disguised as the amiable Mrs. Jonas. As Cara has aptly described her, she was really crafty!

Mr. Logan, Dom's dad and my dad joined us in the basement and looking at my dad's face beaming with excitement, I knew we had already achieved our target. I was right, that is precisely what they announced to us. Dom's dad deposited the money in his safe after signing in the accounts register and my dad and Mr. Logan signed as witnesses. What was wonderful was that we still had one more day to go. Jude suggested that the extra money could be put into a building fund to benefit our towns. The Super and Mr. Logan approved of his suggestion and said they would put it across to the finance committee of the three towns. The last day of the fete was only hours away and we needed as much sleep as we could catch to regain our energy.

CHAPTER 22

I woke up to the brightest and the most beautiful morning of this summer. The past week had gone by like a dream. We had planned to take turns today and play a few games and also take part in some of the events. We were relaxed and could really enjoy ourselves as we had already achieved our target. I had a very good feeling about how things would turn out today. My instincts always guided me in the right direction. Even the weather indicated that it would be a great day. We were to meet directly at the 'Helpline tower' at 10:00 a.m. My mom was hosting a baking competition and I had offered to help her set up things. We left at 9:00 a.m. after attending the 8:00 a.m. service at our local church.

Cara, Mignonne, Dom and Jude were already at the venue where my mom was to conduct the competition. It was a silent pact we had and I did not need to request their help. We always looked out for one another. It was not surprising to see our new friends SP Jensen and Mr. Logan arrive shortly after. The Super told us that Mrs. Brown was under control and seemed docile and calm at the moment. He had asked the lady constable to continue to sedate her as the police department doctor had advised him to do so. He told us that Mr. Brown was less delirious and he would try and question him in the evening. The fingerprint analysis was underway and the report would be faxed to the Super on Monday. SP Jensen said we would have to wait for a day or two to get a clearer picture on the motive for the attempted murder. He was certain it had something to do with the jewels. However, without evidence he did not have a case.

As it was the last day and also a Sunday, the events planned for the day were all the more interesting and spectacular. Dom's dad and my dad had to count the money every half hour and deposit it in the safe. We had anticipated a crowd of a thousand and five hundred people but we noticed that the crowd was almost double. We had enough of manpower to manage the various stalls and there was more than enough food to go around. Our committee members had done their homework very well and had anticipated that we would have a full house as it was the last day of the fete as well as it being a Sunday. It was amazing how well they handled the crowd as if they were professional event managers.

The volley ball match was the penultimate event of the day. The match was very tough and both our town and the second town put up a really good fight. It was a close match and we won by just two points. As it was also the last event that was being rated, our town also bagged the 'Championship cup'. The week had come to an end and that too, so soon. It had been an incredible experience for all of us. The final event of the day proved to be the most spectacular!

Jude had a surprise in store for all the patrons. He had organized a special ceremony so that the fete could be officially closed by the Mayor. The 'closing ceremony' of the fete had performances by the people of the three sister towns, who had made it big in the city. It was heartening to know that though they were celebrities they did not forget their roots and were proud to be a part of their town's festivities. Jude had sent an open invitation to all of them via our social website. They had acknowledged his invitation but, he had never expected them to make it for the occasion on account of their busy schedules. He was thrilled to see them. The patrons were overjoyed.

Jude arranged for all of them to be seated on a special stage where the 'event of the day' was held. He then requested the heads of the various committees to felicitate them. We had artists, people from the film industry, singers, choreographers, head honchos of corporate firms and others from various fields who had all had made it a point to be present.

The most wonderful thing of all was that the bigwigs of the entertainment industry did not hesitate to climb on stage and perform for us. They did it as their contribution to the town, apart from the hefty donation they had given towards the repairs. I knew the people of our towns would treasure the memory of this fete for years to come. The Mayor thanked all the patrons, the well wishers and the celebrities. He once again, thanked Jude and all of us for putting forth the concept of the fete and organizing it.

I had never felt so fulfilled in my life! The success of the fete proved that it only took a little determination, planning and co-operation to put together an event like this. There was not a single committee who did not succeed in achieving their individual targets because, Jude, had anticipated and ironed out all the problems they could have faced. I was sure he would make it really 'big' in the corporate world someday. It would make us really proud that one of our dear friends had done so well for himself.

That night I slept as soon as my head touched my pillow and had dreams of dancing with all the celebrities and serving them gourmet food.

CHAPTER 23

The Super had visited Mr. Brown the previous evening before the volley ball match and had managed to speak with him. He told SP Jensen he could not recall anything as he was asleep when the attack had taken place. On gently questioning him further, the Super had learnt that Mr. Brown could vaguely remember feeling a little breathless while he was asleep. He also recollected some kind of odour but, could not identify it. He was certain that his wife was at home at that time. He had still not asked to see her so, the Super asked him about her. Mr. Brown turned red in the face with anger and started shaking. As his condition was still not stable, SP Jensen at once called the nurse and requested her to give him some medication to calm him down.

The Super gave us this information on the day after the fete. As it was Monday he was sure to receive the information regarding the fingerprints from his friend, the CP.

Mrs. Brown was still being sedated and had a meeting with her lawyer at 4:00 p.m. SP Jensen said that we would have a clearer picture once he questioned Mr. Brown again about his relationship with his wife. No one had attempted an attack on the jeweller nor had anyone tried to rob the coupon counter at the fete. The policemen were instructed to continue guarding the jeweller's shop. It did not seem as if Mrs. Brown had an accomplice unless, she had deliberately told him to stay away. Only time would reveal her motive to murder her husband. We had only ten days till school reopened, and I was eager that the case be solved by then.

The fingerprints report was sent to the Super at 10:00 a.m. The shocking news was that the prints were a perfect match to a felon called Mr. Smith, wanted for theft and murder in six States. The picture sent was that of a bearded man with a thick set of eyebrows, sunken eyes and cheeks. The CP had said he would send his officers from the Homicide section to investigate.

I wondered whether the prints were that of Mrs. Brown's accomplice. The case was getting more complicated and interesting at the same time with the new development.

The Super had visited Mr. Brown in the morning. He was very glad to see SP Jensen. He also seemed to be in a better frame of mind. They got talking and in the course of the conversation, the Super asked him, where he had met his wife and how long since they were married. He learnt that Mr. Brown had married just a month ago and had met his wife at a local pub when he had gone to visit some friends in the city. She had approached him and introduced herself and in the course of the conversation found out about his profession. After that day they met everyday and at the end of his visit, she proposed marriage. He was overjoyed and accepted her proposal. They got married the very next day in a small ceremony which was conducted by a minister she knew very well. Besides them the only ones present were two witnesses. Mr. Brown had never in his wildest dreams expected to return home from his visit to the city with a bride. The most important information he gave the Super was that he always felt drowsy after every meal. It was as if he was drugged but only sufficiently so that he could get on with his regular chores and work. The disappearance of the jewels also had taken place just two days after he had resumed work. There was an inflection in Mr. Brown's voice when he spoke about his work.

The Super saw that it was the right time to probe further as Mr. Brown too seemed to want to tell him more about his involvement in the case. The Super asked if he wanted a lawyer present and also asked permission for his statement to be recorded. Mr. Brown told the SP that he was too stressed to continue to cover his tracks and would like to come clean. He also permitted the Super to record his statement. The Super set up his video camera and recorded the statement.

Mr. Brown told the Super that ever since he was married, his new bride had seemed to have suddenly changed in her manner towards him. She was always ill and kept asking him to bring home money or at least borrow money for her treatment. She pulled out a file which stated that she needed to be operated and would survive only if the operation took place. She had also gently asked him to get hold of some of the jewels when there was no one around. Mr. Brown had told her it was impossible for him to rob the jewels as the security was very tight and the employees were always checked when they left for home. That is when she had come out with an ingenious plan. She told him to pretend to work overtime and at the first opportunity, she asked him to grab some of the jewels from the tumbling barrel. Once he had managed to do that, she had asked him to ingest the jewels by putting them in an inflatable bag which was made of a material that was insoluble.

Mr. Brown was not comfortable carrying out the plan but, he was so in love with his new bride and concerned about her ailment that he had agreed to do it. The opportunity presented itself when he was asked by the jeweller to cut a diamond and requested to complete the work on that day itself as the customer needed it urgently. All the other workers had left and he was still at work when he thought of carrying out his plan. He completed the work and quietly advanced to the tumbling barrel chisel still in hand. In his hurry, he dropped the chisel in the barrel. He panicked and went to retrieve it and that was how he got burnt as he had not worn any protective gear. The workshop had also resounded with the noise and he had quickly wiped the chisel dry and left the workshop. He had not returned to the workshop as the jeweller had decided to close down the manufacturing unit after the jewels had mysteriously disappeared. Mr. Brown swore he had not been successful and had nothing to do with the theft. The Super believed him because the jewels were with us. We had also figured out how the jewels had reached our end of the beach.

The reason Mr. Brown seemed so annoyed with his wife was because she had begun nagging him after that day and had forced him to go around asking people to sponsor her surgery. She had drawn a map and had asked him to walk along the stretch of beach of the neighbouring town and check various drainage outlets. She told him that he would find the jewels. He was very upset at her lack of concern for his well being for she did not seem to care even though he had almost lost his hand due to the burn. For a gem cutter, his hands were most precious as they provided him his livelihood. Mr. Brown told the Super that he regretted his impulsive marriage and said he would advise everyone against making a hasty decision especially where marriage was concerned. He had got carried away by his wife's glib talk and the affection she had showered on him before they got married. The Super felt very sorry for him and was certain he was telling the truth. He reassured him that all would be well in the end. As there were no more questions to be asked as Mr. Brown had revealed all that he knew with utmost sincerity, the SP returned home. He called Jude and told him that he would meet us in an hour to give us an update. He also informed Jude that his friend the CP was sending two of his finest officers to help him when he questioned Mrs. Brown.

The officers from the Homicide department arrived and accompanied SP Jensen to interrogate Mrs. Brown. She was resting and did not seem at all perturbed on seeing the police officers. The lawyer had already spoken with her and Mrs. Brown had revealed nothing. She maintained that she was innocent. The lawyer was also present during the interrogation. The Super asked Mrs. Brown where she was from and how she had met Mr. Brown. She also repeated whatever her husband had said. He asked her where she was on the night her husband was attacked. She said she had gone to a friend's house. The Super knew that it was not true as his men had been watching the place. As she was from the city, she was a stranger to the townspeople and had not made a single friend in her month long stay. She must have been too busy plotting and observing the people so that she could escape disguised as one of them when the time came. The people from the Homicide division then showed her the picture of Mr. Smith. The minute she looked at it, her face contorted and she started writhing as if in pain. Her body stiffened and suddenly she stood up and took a stance like a man.

Her entire demeanor underwent a transformation and it was as if she was now playing the part of a man. The officers asked her who Mr. Smith was and she told them in a male voice it was her name. They questioned her about the murders and she told them how she had cleverly carried out each one of them without ever getting caught. The Super realized that Mrs. Brown was leading them to think that she was a split personality. All along she had played the card of being very frail and ill. Now that she had been arrested, she was trying a new angle. If she went with the insanity plea in the courtroom, she would be institutionalized and would perhaps be released after a few years. The sentence for murder on the other hand would be life imprisonment or the death penalty. Though the Super did not get taken in by her behaviour and was certain that she was a cold and calculating criminal, he would have to gather more evidence to prove it.

SP Jensen doubled the security and kept Mrs. Brown restrained by giving her a stronger dose of sedatives. The doctor who had examined her and conducted a blood test on her found her to be in perfect health. There was no indication of the illness she had claimed she was suffering from. That was just a cover she had used to put us off track and it had worked like a dream on her husband, too. I remember the Super giving her some money to help with her expenses the first time we had met her.

The Super and the officers from the Homicide division and the officers from both the precincts searched the house. As we were not in danger, SP Jensen asked us to accompany them. He had only instructed us not to touch anything as that would mean tampering with the evidence. All of us wore gloves so that we did not leave our fingerprints anywhere. The officers conducted a thorough search but did not find anything. Mignonne as usual, wandered around as she was very curious and loved to observe people at work. Everything interested her! She noticed that one part of the wall of the room upstairs was a shade different from the other part. She called the Super and pointed it out.

The Super called his men and asked them to check it out. Once again our dear 'gadget princess' had noticed a very important detail. The men tapped the wall and found it was hollow. They noticed there was a small groove in the wall which when examined happened to be a tiny doorknob. They gave it a tug and the hollow wall opened to reveal a flight of stairs leading downstairs to a cellar. We followed them to the cellar. In less than five minutes, the police had not only obtained enough evidence to put Mrs. Brown away for a long time but also had found the route through which she had escaped.

The courtroom was packed with all the people of the town. Mrs. Brown was brought before the judge where she confessed to having attempted to murder her husband by cutting open his stomach as she believed that he had ingested the jewels and wanted to keep them for himself. The evidence was presented to the judge. Mrs. Brown seemed to have been very proud of her intellect and had documented every murder she had committed. She would seek out lonely people at pubs and bars strike a conversation with them, gain their confidence and then murder them for money or would get them to steal for her after which she murdered them. She was a trained make-up artist and had used her skill to disguise herself. Every time she had made her escape she had dressed as someone whom everyone was familiar with. She was confident of not being caught as the police were always looking for a bearded man with thick eyebrows, sunken eyes and cheeks that was why she never wore gloves and brazenly left her fingerprints at the scene of the crime. This time she had donned the garb of Mrs. Jonas and had Cara not noticed her and the real Mrs. Jonas at the fete, she would have made her escape once again.

She had unwittingly helped us with the last part of the puzzle when she told us how she had tampered with the pipes and had put corrosive material on both the fresh water pipe and the drainage pipe and attached a pipe to connect them. As she had worked on this in the night, she had failed to do a thorough job. This was her backup plan which Mr. Brown did not know of. She had found that he was too committed to his work and doubted he would ever rob the jewels. Finally the mystery of the narrow length of pipe which was handed over to Mr. Logan along with the two sections of corroded pipes was solved. The drainage water would have never entered the fresh water pipeline. How unscrupulous she was! She had not given a second thought about how this could endanger the health of the townspeople. Mr. Logan and his PWD department could rest easy. It had never been a case of negligence on their part. She brazenly told us that it was on account of this that Mr. Brown's took those long walks along the sea-shore of the third town. He had been looking for the jewels and searching all the outlets in the hope of finding them without drawing attention to himself. She had miscalculated where the jewels would land as she had worked in the dark. She had a very high opinion of her capabilities and had never thought she could have misjudged the stretch of beach it would be found. Also, she herself had fallen ill due to the contaminated water and by the time she had recovered, we had already begun our investigation and were on our guard.

The reason she had not visited the hospital was because she was unaware that Mr. Brown had survived the attack. She had responded to the District Attorney's question of how she had managed to overpower Mr. Brown who was twice her size. She proudly replied how she had suggested that her husband rest before dinner. Then when he was asleep she had pressed a cloth dipped in chloroform over his nose, after which she cut open his stomach.

When the judge asked her if she wanted to say anything in her defense, she replied that the only remorse she felt was that Mr. Brown had not been able to ingest the jewels and had failed to carry out her carefully thought-out plan. She also insisted that he had found the jewels and had kept them for himself and so should be arrested as he was a thief. Of course as we had found the culprit, the Mayor had already announced to the entire town that the jewels had been found by us so, nobody reacted to her statement.

We had returned all the jewels along-with the inventory made by Mr. Sinclair to the jeweller who was overjoyed as each and every gem that he had lost had been found and that too in pristine condition. He made a hefty donation towards the building fund. He also rewarded the five of us by giving each of us a beautifully studded jewelled finger-ring. Mignonne was the happiest as she had got her 'REWARD'.

The judge sentenced Mrs. Brown to life imprisonment in a maximum security correction centre and also suggested a psychiatric evaluation of her personality. I had never thought such a frail and petite looking person could have turned out so calculative and capable of committing several murders of the first degree. Well, appearances are deceptive and Mrs. Brown was an expert at deceit. The Homicide officers handcuffed her and led her to the armoured vehicle which was waiting to take her to the correction centre. Mr. Brown was still in hospital and was not present for the trial. It would be too much for him to take as he was still recouping. The news would have to be broken to him gently. His well wishers would certainly take care of him as he had no relatives. Our dear Super was sure to arrange for a house-keeper so that he was well taken care of.

What a pity though that Megan, Karl and Jodie had missed all the excitement! They were sure to have had a good time at camp but, nothing could compare with all that we had been part of during this summer vacation. We had so much to tell them! Fortunately, we had most of it video-taped. They were to return from camp the following day.

What an amazing holiday it had been. It was action packed from day one when Mignonne had found the diamond – 'spectra'. We had gained a firsthand experience of how a police investigation is conducted. We learnt about the working of the PWD. The planning and execution of the fete helped us contribute to our town in a big way. We got to meet celebrities and were felicitated in their august presence. Mr. Brown survived the attempt on his life. We helped nab a wanted felon! We were also the proud owners of beautiful jewelled rings a memento of our amazing adventure!!!! How much better could it have been! It was and I am sure will always remain my best summer ever!!!!